the further adventures of
SHERLOCK HOLMES

THE SCROLL OF THE DEAD

AVAILABLE NOW FROM TITAN BOOKS

THE FURTHER ADVENTURES OF SHERLOCK HOLMES
THE ECTOPLASMIC MAN
Daniel Stashower
ISBN: 9781848564923

THE FURTHER ADVENTURES OF SHERLOCK HOLMES
THE VEILED DETECTIVE
David Stuart Davies
ISBN: 9781848564909

THE FURTHER ADVENTURES OF SHERLOCK HOLMES
THE WAR OF THE WORLDS
Manly Wade Wellman & Wade Wellman
ISBN: 9781848564916

COMING SOON FROM TITAN BOOKS

THE FURTHER ADVENTURES OF SHERLOCK HOLMES
THE MAN FROM HELL
Barrie Roberts
ISBN: 9781848565081

THE FURTHER ADVENTURES OF SHERLOCK HOLMES
THE STALWART COMPANIONS
H. Paul Jeffers
ISBN: 9781848565098

THE SCROLL OF THE DEAD

DAVID STUART DAVIES

TITAN BOOKS

THE FURTHER ADVENTURES OF SHERLOCK HOLMES
THE SCROLL OF THE DEAD

ISBN: 9781848564930

Published by
Titan Books
A division of Titan Publishing Group Ltd
144 Southwark St
London
SE1 0UP

First Titan edition: October 2009
10 9 8 7 6 5 4 3 2 1

Visit our website:
www.titanbooks.com

What did you think of this book? We love to hear from our readers. Please email us at: readerfeedback@titanemail.com, or write to us at the above address.

To receive advance information, news, competitions, and exclusive Titan offers online, please register as a member by clicking the 'sign up' button on our website: www.titanbooks.com

A CIP catalogue record for this title is available from the British Library.

Printed in the USA.

To
Freda & Tony
Cherished Chums

Narrator's Note

The details of several incidents in this complex investigation only came to my knowledge once the case was closed. Using the information that was furnished to me, I have taken the liberty of dramatising these incidents in order that the reader may be presented with a coherent and cohesive narrative.

John H. Watson

Prologue

Fate has a strange way of creating a series of events which initially appear to be in no way connected and yet which, with hindsight, can be discerned as cunning links in an arcane chain. My friend, Mr Sherlock Holmes, was usually very astute not only in observing, but also in predicting these matters. Indeed, it was part of his skill as a detective. However, in the affair of the Scroll of the Dead even he, at first, failed to see the relationship between a weird and singular set of occurrences which involved us in one of our most challenging cases.

To relate the story in full, I must refer to my notes detailing a period some twelve months prior to the murders and the theft of the Scroll. The first link in our chain was forged in early May, the year following Holmes' return from his wanderings abroad after the Reichenbach incident. It was a dark and dismal Tuesday, as I remember it: one of those days which makes you think you have been deceived by the previous day's sunshine and that spring has not really arrived after all. I had been at my club for most of the afternoon playing billiards with Thurston. I left at five, just as the murky day was crawling its way to solemn evening, and returned to Baker Street. I poured myself a stiff brandy, a compensation for losing so badly to Thurston, and sat opposite my friend beside our fire. Holmes, who had been turning the pages of a newspaper in a desultory fashion, suddenly threw it down with a sigh and addressed me in a languid and casual manner.

'Would you care to accompany me this evening, Watson?' he murmured, a mischievous twinkle lighting his eye. 'I have an appointment in Kensington, where I shall be communicating with the dead.'

'Certainly, my dear fellow,' I replied easily, sipping my brandy and stretching my legs before the fire.

Holmes caught my impassive expression and burst into a fit of laughter. 'A touch, an undeniable touch,' he chortled. 'Bravo, Watson. You are developing a nice facility for dissembling.'

'I have had a good teacher.'

He raised his eyebrows in mock surprise.

'However,' I added pointedly, 'it is more likely that I am growing used to your outrageous statements.'

He beamed irritatingly and rubbed his hands. 'Outrageous statements. Tut, tut. I speak naught but the truth.'

'Communicating with the dead,' I remarked with incredulity.

'A séance, my dear fellow.'

'Surely you are joking,' said I.

'Indeed not. I have an appointment with Mr Uriah Hawkshaw, medium, clairvoyant, and spiritual guide, this very evening at nine-thirty sharp. He assures me that he will endeavour to make contact with my dear departed Aunt Sophie. I may take along a friend.'

'I was not aware you had an Aunt Sophie… Holmes, there is more to this than meets the eye.'

'Astute as ever,' Holmes grinned, as he slipped his watch from his waistcoat pocket. 'Ah, just time for a wash and a shave before I leave. Are you game?'

* * *

Some time later, as we rattled through the darkened London streets in a hansom, Holmes offered the proper explanation for this evening's strange excursion.

'I am performing a favour for my brother, Mycroft. A member of his staff, Sir Robert Hythe, has recently lost his son in a boating accident. The lad was the apple of his father's eye and his death has affected Sir Robert badly. Apparently he was just coming to terms with his tragic loss, when this Hawkshaw character contacted him and claimed that he was receiving spirit messages from the boy.'

'What nonsense!'

'My sentiments too, Watson. But to a grieving father such claims are straws grasped instinctively. In despair, logic is forgotten and replaced by wild hopes and dreams. Apparently Mr Uriah Hawkshaw is a most convincing rogue…'

'Rogue?'

'So Mycroft believes. He is one of these Spiritualist charlatans who milk the weak and the bereaved of their wealth in return for a gobbledegook puppet show. Mycroft is concerned as to how far this situation may develop. Hythe is privy to many of the government's secrets and, purely on a personal level, my brother is keen that the fellow should not be misled any further.'

'What is your role in the matter?'

'I am to unmask this ghost-maker for what he is – a fraud and a cheat.'

'How?'

'Oh, that should be easy enough. According to my research there are many ways in which these individuals can be exposed. Really, Watson, it has been a most instructive venture. I have thoroughly enjoyed delving into this dark subject. My studies have led me down several learned and diverse avenues, including a visit to Professor Abraham Jordan, expert in the languages of the North American Indian. It is now clear to me that in order for the unmasking to be achieved convincingly, it has to be done while the dissembler is about his nefarious business – in performance, as it were – with his unfortunate victims in attendance.'

'Sir Robert will be present this evening?'

'Indeed. These entertainments are not exclusive. The vultures assemble many carrion at one sitting for their pickings. I am Ambrose Trelawney, by the way. My beloved Aunt Sophie passed away just over a year ago. No doubt tonight I shall receive a message from the old dear.' Holmes chuckled in the darkness.

I did not share my friend's amusement in this matter. Not for one moment did I countenance the existence of these roving spirits with an appetite to communicate with the carnate world, but at the same time I sympathised, indeed empathised, with those sad creatures who, in the depths of despair at losing someone dear to them, stretched their arms out into the darkness for solace and comfort. Holmes, it seemed, had not contemplated the psychological damage that could be incurred by the destruction of such beliefs. In common with these charlatans, he was only concerned with his own magic. For myself, as I sat back in the swaying cab, I could not help but think of my own dear Mary and what I would give to hear her sweet voice again.

Within a short time we were traversing the select highways of Kensington. As I gazed from the window of the cab at the elegant houses, Holmes caught my train of thought.

'Oh yes, there is money in the ghost business, Watson. Mr Hawkshaw lives the life of a wealthy man.'

Moments later we drew up in front of a large Georgian town dwelling which bore the name 'Frontier Lodge' on a brass plaque on the gate post. Holmes paid the cabby and rang the bell. We were admitted by a tall negro manservant of repellent aspect attired in an ill-fitting dress suit. He spoke in a harsh, rasping tone as though he had been forbidden to raise his voice above a whisper. He took our coats and showed us into 'the sanctum': this was a gloomy room at the back of the house, illuminated only by candles. As we entered, a gaunt, sandy-haired man in his fifties came forward and grasped Holmes' hand.

'Mr Trelawney,' he said in an unpleasant, unctuous tone.

Holmes nodded gravely. 'Good evening, Mr Hawkshaw,' he replied in a halting manner, bowing his head briefly as he spoke.

The performance had begun.

'I am so glad that my secretary was able to accommodate you at our sitting. The vibrations have been building all day; I sense that we shall make some very special contacts this evening.'

'I do hope so,' replied Holmes with a trembling eagerness.

Hawkshaw glanced quizzically at me over my friend's shoulders. I saw in those watery orbs a kind of steely avarice which disgusted me. 'And this is...?' he enquired.

Before I had chance to respond, Holmes answered for me. 'This is my manservant, Hamish. He is my constant companion.' Holmes smiled sweetly in my direction and added, 'But he does not say very much.'

With as much grace as I could muster, I gave Hawkshaw a nod of acknowledgement, before glowering at Holmes, who ignored my glance and continued to beam warmly.

'Let me introduce you to my other... visitor.' Hawkshaw hesitated over the last word as though it was not quite the appropriate term to use but, on the other hand, he was well aware that the term 'client' would sound gauche and mercenary. He turned and beckoned from the shadows a lean, distinguished-looking man with a fine thatch of grey hair and a neat military moustache.

'Sir Robert Hythe, this is Mr Ambrose Trelawney.' Holmes shook Sir Robert's hand and the knight lowered his head in vague greeting. With a distracted air, Sir Robert shook my hand also, but Hawkshaw failed to proffer an introduction. It was clear that as a mere manservant, and not a wealthy client, I was of little importance to the medium.

'We have great hopes of reaching Sir Robert's son tonight,' crooned Hawkshaw, his face mobile and sympathetic, with eyes that remained cold and stony.

'Indeed,' remarked Holmes quietly, observing Sir Robert closely. The man was obviously embarrassed by Hawkshaw's statement and his sensitive features registered a moment of pain before they fell once more into vacant repose. I had heard something of Sir Robert's notable military and political career and therefore it struck me as odd, incongruous even, that this courageous, decent, and astute individual should have fallen so easily into the avaricious clutches of a creature like Hawkshaw. Such, I supposed, was the weakening power of grief that it dulled one's reasoning faculties.

As there came an uneasy pause in the stilted conversation, the door swung open and a dark-haired woman in a wine-red gown entered and hurried to Hawkshaw's side. 'My dear, our final guest has arrived.'

The medium beamed with pleasure and turned, as did we all, to gaze upon the stranger who stood on the threshold of the room. He was a young man, not yet out of his twenties, tall and with a certain plumpness of face. He was dressed in a black velvet jacket, with a large floppy bow at the neck, and his long blond hair flowed down to touch the collar of his jacket.

'Gentlemen,' said Hawkshaw grandly, 'allow me to introduce Mr Sebastian Melmoth.'

The pale youth's face twisted into a thin smile of greeting. I had heard something of this Melmoth. He had the reputation of being a dissolute dandy, one of the effete admirers of the decadent Oscar Wilde. There were tales of his indulgences in various unpleasant acts of debauchery, even rumours that he had dabbled in the Black Arts and other such abominations – but this was the gossip at my club in the late hours when the billiard cues were back in their racks and the cigars and brandy were being savoured. Looking upon that soft, alabaster face now, sensitive, almost beautiful in the dim light, it seemed to have all the vulnerability and expectancy of youth; but there was something about the large fleshy lips and arrogant sneer which suggested cruelty and disdain.

Perfunctory greetings were exchanged and I briefly held Melmoth's cold, languid flesh as we shook hands. Unlike Holmes, I often judge my fellow man not by the coat cuff or the trouser knee, but by instincts; and, irrational as instincts may seem to my scientific friend, I know that not only did I neither like nor trust Mr Sebastian Melmoth, I also sensed that there was something intrinsically evil about him.

Mrs Hawkshaw, for she it was in the wine-coloured dress, placed a wax cylinder on the gramophone, and the faint, ethereal music of some composer unknown to me wafted into the air. All but one candle was extinguished and we were invited to take our places. The medium himself sat at the head of the table on a dark, ornate carver chair shaped like some medieval throne. His wife was seated beside him: I was next to her, then Sir Robert, Holmes, and by him, Melmoth.

There was a minute's silence during which no one spoke. We sat mute and expectant in the Stygian gloom. Despite the one yellow prick of flame, my eyes could make out little but the pale, strained and expectant faces around the table. Eventually, the scratchy music died away and Mrs Hawkshaw addressed us.

'Gentlemen, tonight my husband will attempt to go beyond the frail boundaries of this earthly life and contact our loved ones who have departed their carnate bodies.' She spoke in flat, monotonous tones as though reciting some dirge. It took me a good deal of effort to contain my indignation at such nonsense.

'I cannot stress too highly that it is imperative you do exactly as I say,' she continued, 'otherwise this meeting will end in failure and you could endanger the life of my husband.'

I glanced up at Hawkshaw. He seemed to be asleep, eyes closed, head lolling on his chest.

'Now, please place your hands on the table and hold hands with those sitting either side of you.' She paused while we obeyed in silent unison.

'Thank you. Now we must wait a while for the spirit guide to come through.'

Sitting in the wavering gloom, I contemplated this ridiculous situation: how sad it was for those individuals who could not accept death's final victory, and how despicable it was for characters like Hawkshaw to exploit their weakness for coin.

We seemed to be sitting there for some ten minutes, listening only to the heavy breathing of Hawkshaw. Indeed, I felt my own eyelids drooping and my body beginning to surrender to sleep also when, suddenly in the darkness, there came the sound of birdsong. It was clear and definite and so close that I could imagine some feathered creature fluttering in a circle around the table, its wings wafting near our faces. The sound was accompanied by a distinct chill in the air which filled the room. The candle guttered wildly, throwing distorting shadows across the pale features of my companions. It gave the eerie impression that their faces were somehow melting, changing and being re-shaped. The intense atmosphere and the darkness were playing tricks with my imagination, as surely they were designed to do. I breathed deeply and shook my head to rid myself of such unpleasant and unrealistic images.

At length, the birdsong died away. As it did so, the gramophone started up once again, filling the chamber with its weird, crackly melody. As we were all holding hands, some unseen force must have set the machine in motion.

'The spirits are working,' intoned Mrs Hawkshaw, as though in answer to the question that was on my lips.

By the feeble glow of the solitary candle, I discerned that the faces of the others were intense, none more so than Holmes, who peered determinedly into the darkness beyond the frail amber pool of illumination. It was as though he expected to see something in the shifting shadows – something tangible. And indeed he did. We all did. There was a strange rustling noise and then I glimpsed in the candlelight a flash of metal. Moments later it came again and then there materialised, hovering over Hawkshaw's head, what appeared to be a brass horn. It shimmered like a mirage in the flickering light.

I glanced back at Holmes: at first a cynical smile had touched his lips, but now he seemed disturbed by what he had seen. His look of concern struck a note of unease in my own breast. Had I been wrong all along to scoff at such matters? Could the dead really communicate with us, the living? My hands grew clammy at the thought.

The horn hovered in the air for a time, moving gently above Hawkshaw's head; then it slowly receded into the darkness, disappearing from sight.

'The spirits are ready to speak,' Mrs Hawkshaw informed us in a hushed monotone.

This simple statement with its awful import struck fear into my heart. The certainties with which I had entered the room had slowly dissipated. I had witnessed inexplicable phenomena and sensed the world of the unreal. What, I wondered, was next?

Hawkshaw, who had been like a dreaming statue, suddenly jerked upright, his eyes wide open and his nostrils flaring. A gagging sound emanated from his mouth and then he bellowed in a deep, dark, alien voice, 'What is it you want from me?'

Hawkshaw answered the question in his own voice. 'Is it Black Cloud?'

There was a pause before the reply came: 'I am Black Cloud, a Chief of the Santee tribe, warrior of the great Sioux nation.'

'Are you our spirit guide for tonight?'

There was a moment's hesitation in this macabre conversation before the strange voice emerged from Hawkshaw once more, his lips hardly moving. 'There are many here who are content and are at peace. They have no messages for the other world.'

'Black Cloud, please help us again as you have done in the past. Our dear friends in the circle here have lost loved ones. They need comfort. They need reassurance.'

'Who is it you seek?'

Mrs Hawkshaw turned to Sir Robert and indicated that he should speak.

With an eagerness which showed no restraint, Sir Robert leaned over the table towards Hawkshaw. 'Nigel. I wish to speak to my son Nigel.'

There was a long pause. I felt my own nerves tensing with expectation, and then there came a sound, soft and gentle like the rustling of silk: as though someone were whispering in the darkness.

'Nigel?' barked Sir Robert in desperate tones.

'Father.' The response was muffled and high-pitched, but unmistakably that of a youth.

A look of surprise etched itself upon the features of Sherlock Holmes. His face slightly forward, he peered desperately into the darkness.

'Nigel, my boy, is it really you?'

'Yes, father.'

Sir Robert closed his eyes and his chest heaved with emotion.

'Don't mourn for me, father,' the epicene voice advised him. 'I am happy here. I am at peace.'

Tears were now running down the knight's face as he struggled to keep his strong emotions in check.

'I must go now, father. Come again and we shall talk further.

Goodbye.' The voice faded and the whispering returned briefly, before that ceased also.

'Nigel, please don't go yet. Stay, please. I have so many questions to ask. Stay, please.'

'The spirits will not be bidden by you. Be content you have made contact. There will be other times.' It was Black Cloud speaking once more.

Before Sir Robert could respond, Holmes addressed the medium. 'Black Cloud, may I ask a question?'

There was an abrupt silence before there was a reply. At length it came in the same dark, stilted delivery. 'You may ask.'

'Black Cloud, you are a chieftain of the Santee? Is that correct?'

'I am.'

Holmes then spoke in a tongue I had never heard before: a guttural, staccato dialect which he enunciated with great deliberation. I presumed that he was speaking the language of the Santee.

When he finished there was an uneasy pause. Holmes repeated a few words in this strange tongue and then reverted to English. 'Come now, do not tell me that you fail to comprehend the tongue of your race,' he prompted with cold authority.

There was no reply from Black Cloud.

'Perhaps then I had better interpret for you. I called you an unscrupulous fraud, Hawkshaw. I detailed the methods by which you achieved your tawdry tricks...'

'Mr Trelawney, please...' This interruption came from Sir Robert.

'Bear with me, sir. Is it not suspicious that a Santee could not understand his own native tongue, the language in which I addressed him?'

As Holmes spoke, Hawkshaw fell head first on the table as in a faint.

'Now see what you have done,' cried the man's wife, leaning over her husband.

'Another diversionary tactic, I have no doubt,' snapped Holmes, leaping from his seat. 'Let us throw some light on the matter, shall we? I noticed the electric switch earlier...' With a deft movement, he flooded the room with bright light. The rest of us were too stunned to move as he swept past the table and pulled back the drapes to reveal the negro manservant cowering there, clasping the brass horn we had earlier seen floating in the air. Behind him the French windows were open. Holmes closed them quickly to prevent the servant's escape.

My friend turned to face us, a grin of triumph on his lips. 'I am sure you all felt the chill at the start of the séance. A window left open is the simple explanation. As for the whispering, the self-operated gramophone, and the floating horn, our friend here simply stepped through the curtains and made the noises, set the machine in motion, while with his black gloves he held the horn where it might be seen and he would not. Isn't that correct?'

The negro, with downcast head, mumbled his agreement.

'As for the rest, a facility for mimicry and ventriloquism are Mr Hawkshaw's only talents. You will admit, Sir Robert, that the voice you heard did not sound very like your son.'

The knight, whose face was drawn and haggard in the bright light, appeared to be in state of shock. 'I suppose... I wanted it to sound like Nigel.'

'Indeed. Wish-fulfilment is the greatest ally of these charlatans.'

'How dare you!' screamed Mrs Hawkshaw, stroking her husband's head. 'See how you've affected him with your slander.'

'I am sure he will make a full recovery,' snapped Holmes, grabbing the collar of Hawkshaw's jacket, jerking him off the table, and slapping him heartily on the back. As he did so, a small metallic object flew from the medium's mouth. 'He's just swallowed one bird too many.'

I picked it up and examined it.

'A cunning device: it's a bird warbler – hence the aviary sounds we experienced earlier.'

'You've been damned clever, sir,' observed Sebastian Melmoth smoothly, lighting up a little black cigar. 'You've performed a great service for us all.'

Holmes gave a little bow and then turned to the medium and his wife who, struggling to come to terms with their exposure, were hugging each other in miserable desperation. 'Now, I suggest you return any monies you have received from these gentlemen, and then it is time to shut up your fake show for good. If I hear of you practising your despicable charades again, it will become a police matter. Is that understood?'

Almost in unison the Hawkshaws nodded dumbly.

Melmoth chuckled merrily. 'You put on a fine show yourself, Mr Trelawney. Bravo.'

Holmes smiled coldly. 'In this instance, the deceivers have been deceived. I am not Mr Trelawney. I am Sherlock Holmes.'

It was a week later when a strange coda to this episode was played out in our Baker Street rooms. It was late, about the time when a man thinks of retiring to bed with a good book. Holmes had spent the evening making a series of notes for a monograph on the uses of photography in the detection of crime and was in a mellow mood. A thin smile had softened his gaunt features during his preoccupations. I was about to bid him goodnight, when our doorbell rang downstairs.

'Too late for a social visit. It must be a client,' said Holmes, verbalising my own thoughts.

Within moments there was a discreet knock at our door and our visitor entered.

It was Sebastian Melmoth.

He was dressed very much in the manner in which we had seen him last and he was clutching a magnum of champagne. Holmes bade him take a seat.

'I am sorry to visit at so late an hour, but it has been my intention for some days to call upon you, Mr Holmes, and this has been my first opportunity.'

My friend slid down in his seat and placed his steepled fingers to his lips. 'I am intrigued,' he said lazily.

Melmoth, almost ignoring my presence, raised the magnum as though it were a trophy. 'A little gift for you, Mr Holmes, in gratitude.' He placed it at my friend's feet.

Holmes raised a questioning eyebrow.

'For exposing that scoundrel, Hawkshaw. I had heard so many good accounts of the fellow that I really believed that I had found the genuine article at last.'

'Your thanks are misplaced, Mr Melmoth. You are neither poor nor bereaved, and therefore any benefits that you received from my little performance at Frontier Lodge are purely coincidental.'

Melmoth's icy cold blue eyes flashed enigmatically and he leaned forward, the young, plump face demonic in the shadow-light. 'Money means little to me, Mr Holmes; and you are quite correct. I am not – at present – bereaved. However, I am most serious in my research, and you have successfully sealed up one avenue of investigation for me.'

I could retain my curiosity no longer. 'May I ask exactly what kind of research you pursue?' I enquired.

Melmoth turned to me as though he had only just become aware of my presence. 'Research into death,' he said softly. 'The life beyond living.'

My puzzled expression prompted him to expand on his reply.

'I am of the new age in scientific thinking, Doctor Watson. Death is a medieval mystery, a mystery that can be solved – *must* be solved. I do not believe that we scrape and scrabble our way along the weary road of life merely to fade into oblivion upon reaching the end. There is more. There *must* be more. Like Oliver Lodge and those of his persuasion, I believe that life, as we know it, is just the beginning – the starting point. I talk not of Heaven as prescribed by the scriptures, that fairyland in the sky, but of a door through which we pass into immortality.'

Warming to his exposition, with flushed cheeks and tense jawline, he rose and threw his arms wide. 'Take a walk into the East End of this city, gentlemen. See the poverty there, the suffering, the open degradation. Human beings living and behaving like animals in the filth and squalor. Is that Life? Come, gentlemen, there has to be more. There is a key. Somewhere there is a key to unlock the secret of it all. You, Mr Holmes, deal with the ills of society; you, Doctor, minister to the ailments of the body. So be it; but I search beyond those petty concerns.'

'You believe that you can alter the natural course of events?' said Holmes.

Melmoth shook his head. 'What you talk of as being natural is only regarded as such out of ignorance. Death is natural, I grant you, but the end of living is not. That the state of being ceases with the arrival of the burial casket is accepted by the naive, because it has never been challenged. No illness known to man would have been cured if someone had not challenged it. We would still be living in caves had there not been those who challenged the accepted beliefs and pushed the boundaries forward. I do not believe death is the end. Its power can and will be conquered.' Suddenly he stopped in mid-flow, as though he realised that perhaps he had said too much. His face broke into a wide, unpleasant smile and his voice dropped to a sibilant whisper like a hissing snake. I assure you, gentlemen, I am correct.'

With this parting remark, he bowed low in a theatrical manner and swept from the room.

'The fellow is mad,' I said, as I heard him clatter down our stairs.

Holmes stared at the burning embers in the grate. 'If only it were as simple as that, Watson.'

One

An Inspector Calls

It has often been said – indeed, I have been one of those who have said it – that Sherlock Holmes, the famous consulting detective, was *the* champion of law and order of his age. However, on reflection, I can state that this is only partly true. Crime did indeed fascinate Holmes, but when it came to the solving of it, he was very selective. I have been present when he has rejected numerous pleas and entreaties to tackle a particular mystery solely on the basis that it was simply not interesting enough. The misdemeanours that intrigued my capricious friend had to bear the hallmark of the *recherché* before he would contemplate involving himself in providing a solution. He loved detective work for its own sake, but the detective work had to pose an unusual conundrum or it presented no challenge.

So it was in the spring of 1896 when, after a very fallow period, he devoured news of criminal activity reported in the daily press in the hope of spotting some intriguing puzzle to satisfy his needs. I would aid him every morning in this pursuit by pointing out what I regarded to be crimes of intellectual interest.

'What you may consider stimulating to the deductive brain, Watson, falls far short of my ideal,' he would comment disparagingly. "Music Hall Artiste Strangled In Dressing Room" poses no cerebral challenge whatsoever. A case of jealousy and intoxication. No doubt even the Scotland Yarders could cope with that one in a day!'

'Have you seen the report in *The Chronicle* of the murder of Sir George Faversham, the noted archaeologist?'

Holmes took his pipe from his mouth and paused. 'Items stolen from the family home?'

'Nothing of real value taken.'

'Ah,' he scoffed. 'Common burglary with homicidal consequences.'

I threw down the paper. 'I give up,' I cried. 'There is obviously nothing that will satisfy you.'

Holmes gave me a weak grin. 'Well, at least we are agreed on that point.' His eye wandered to the drawer in his bureau where I knew he still kept the neat Morocco case containing the hypodermic syringe.

'And that is not the answer either,' I snapped.

For a moment Holmes looked surprised, and then a dreamy smile touched his countenance. He realised that I was playing him at his own game by reading his thoughts. The idea amused him so much that he burst out with a roar of laughter. His hilarity was so contagious that soon I was laughing along with him. So enwrapped were we in our own amusement that we failed to take notice of the insistent knock at our sitting room door. Moments later, it opened hesitantly and Inspector Hardcastle of the Yard stood on our threshold. Holmes had worked with Hardcastle on a couple of investigations in the past, notably the 'Disappearing Chinese Laundry Affair'. He was a dour Yorkshireman who was methodical and thorough, rather than inspired, in his police work. He appeared most discomfited by our abandoned behaviour.

'If I have called at an inconvenient moment, gentlemen...' he said, bristling somewhat, unsure whether he was the cause of our amusement.

'Not at all, Hardcastle,' cried my friend, still chortling. 'It is always a pleasure to receive a visit from one of my friends in the official force.' He waved the Scotland Yarder to a chair. 'Sit down, my dear fellow, and don't look so disheartened. Weeks of inactivity have lightened my brain. You are indeed a sight for sore eyes, especially if you have a case for us.'

The inspector, uncertainty still clouding his features, did as he was bidden. He was a tall, beefy man whose great oval face was beset with large, grey, mournful eyes and a broken nose. His black hair, plastered with cream, looked as though it had just been dropped on his head. Clutching his bowler tightly in his large hands, he sat awkwardly in the chair opposite us.

'You *do* have a case for us?' enquired Holmes languidly, his mood changing rapidly.

'Something I thought might interest you,' said Hardcastle, his equilibrium still not restored.

'I hope it's not something already reported in the papers,' observed Holmes, relighting his pipe with a glowing cinder from the fire. 'It's not the strangled magician at Henty's Music Hall?'

'It most certainly is not,' snapped Hardcastle indignantly. 'Young Kingsley is on that case. I put my money on Roland Reilly, the "Irish Vagabond with a Voice of Gold".'

'I am sure you are right. I have heard that when in drink he has a towering rage. In the confined world of the music hall artiste, the smallest slights and petty jealousies become magnified beyond all reason. I wonder that there isn't a blood bath every night.'

Hardcastle looked curiously at my friend, striving to ascertain whether Holmes was being serious or still gently teasing him.

'Come, come,' said Holmes, spinning his hand as a conductor might to increase the speed of the music, 'let us hear about your case, Hardcastle.'

'There's been a break-in at the British Museum.'

'Is that all?' groaned Holmes, slumping back in the chair.

'There's more to it than that.'

'There had better be. What was stolen: some medieval pottery, or some gewgaws belonging to Henry VIII, perhaps?'

'I'll come to that in a moment. It was a very professional job. A two man operation.'

'How do you know?'

The Inspector's face lit up. 'Because they were foolish enough to leave clues behind, Mr Holmes. We found two sets of muddy footprints near the scene of the crime and, before you ask, they could not have been anyone else's because the floor is mopped clean after closing time.'

Holmes held his hands up in mock surrender. 'Two men it is then, Hardcastle.'

'The crib-cracker and the expert, I should guess.'

'Expert?' I asked.

'Yes, Doctor Watson. Whoever it was knew exactly what he wanted. He had the whole ruddy museum to go at and just the one thing was taken.'

Holmes leaned forward a little, interested now. 'What was that "one thing"?'

'Some papyrus document – a scroll, I think.'

'Ah, from the Egyptology room.'

'That's right. Full of those old mummies and dog-headed statues and the like.'

'And,' said Holmes 'various gold trinkets and other very precious *objets d'art* which would have been far easier and more profitable to dispose of than a crumbling old document.'

'Precisely, Mr Holmes.'

'Well, Watson, what does this suggest to you?'

'A collector. The item to be added to his private collection, for his own personal viewing.'

My friend beamed. 'A very determined collector.'

'More determined than you'd think,' said Hardcastle. 'Determined enough to kill for the booty.'

'Who?'

'The night security guard.'

'How?'

'Shot in the head at point blank range.'

'Really.'

'With a Derringer pistol.'

'How can you be so sure?' I asked.

In answer, Hardcastle fumbled in his pocket and pulled out a dark velvet bag fastened with a draw-string at the top. Opening the bag, he allowed the contents to slip onto the small table by Holmes. It was a small silver Derringer pistol which sparkled in the firelight. 'The murderer dropped it while making his escape.'

'Careless of him,' said Holmes, taking a long-stemmed clay pipe from the rack on the mantelpiece. Slipping the stem through the trigger guard, he lifted up the pistol to examine it. 'An expensive weapon... chased silver... a recent purchase...' He murmured these comments more to himself than to us.

'I remembered about your own system for checking fingerprints, Mr Holmes,' said Hardcastle eagerly. 'That's how you managed to lay a trap for Fu Wong, but I reckon you won't find any on that gun.'

'Of course not. This fellow would have worn gloves.' He sniffed the weapon, which had a finely-tooled brown leather grip, and then examined the barrel. 'Fired just the once. Not the kind of firearm usually associated with burglary and the class of crib-crackers we've encountered before, eh, Watson?'

'It's a ladies' gun,' I sniffed.

'But it does a man's job.' Holmes took it over to the window and, retrieving his lens from the bureau, scrutinised the Derringer closely. At length he returned to his chair. Slipping the pistol into the velvet bag, he handed it back to the inspector.

'Anything, Mr Holmes?'

Holmes pursed his lips and shook his head. 'Very little. The owner is a youngish man with blond hair, has expensive tastes, is somewhat extravagant in nature, is arrogant, and extremely confident. And he is probably mentally unstable.'

The inspector's eyes widened. 'How on earth do you reach those conclusions?'

'A fine blond hair caught in the trigger guard gives me the colouring and the age, and there is the faint aroma of gentlemen's *eau de toilette* still lingering about the the leather grip. The owner obviously handled the weapon while his fingers were still moist with the perfume and it has soaked into the fine crevices of the tooled leather. For so persistent an aroma to remain, this particular fragrance could not have been purchased for less than fifty shillings a bottle, which indicates both the expensive taste and the extravagant nature. The fact that there was only one bullet in the gun suggests our young villain was supremely confident that only one bullet was required for the deed. That smacks of remarkable arrogance also. The probability that this fellow adorned himself with expensive *eau de toilette* before going out to commit a horrid crime implies that he views murder almost as a social event – which suggests to me a certain element of mental instability.'

'Extraordinary,' murmured Hardcastle. I was unsure whether he was referring to Holmes' ability to fill in so many details about the murderer from a brief examination of his gun or to the character of the killer as my friend had described him.

'Those few details may be of assistance as the case progresses, but at present they do not get us very far. I suspect that the real help will come from discovering more about the nature of the item that was stolen.'

Hardcastle appeared unconvinced. 'As I said, Mr Holmes: it was just some old papyrus document covered with ancient writing.'

'Hieroglyphics,' I said.

The policeman's face crumpled with distaste. 'So I gather, Doctor. I must admit I'm much more at home with the theft of plate, stolen gems, or a straightforward shoot 'em or stab 'em murder case.'

Holmes' eyes sparkled mischievously. 'And it has taken you approximately forty-eight hours to discover that you are out of your depth in the matter. Ah, don't deny it, Inspector. The deterioration of the cordite in the gun-barrel tells me that it is some two to three days since it was fired; and, quite honestly, old chap, the depth of the furrows on your brow speaks of a weary problem, one that has been with you for several days and not one that has been thrust upon you overnight. It is Monday morning now. I would estimate that the robbery took place on Friday night. Am I correct?'

Hardcastle nodded dumbly.

'But there has been no mention in the press of the crime,' said I.

'We managed to keep it out of the papers,' Hardcastle replied. 'We needed the time to check up on the various dealers who handle this kind of specialised merchandise before the press got wind of it.'

' "Dusty" Morrison and his ilk?'

The inspector nodded. 'That's right, Mr Holmes. We followed up all the known leads both in and out of the Rogues' Gallery, but we hit a brick wall with all of 'em.'

'How valuable is this document?' I asked.

Hardcastle shrugged. 'They can't really put a price on it. To you or me, Doctor, it would be pretty worthless, but to a connoisseur of these kinds of things, it's priceless.' Suddenly the policeman strained forward, his face twisting into a pained grimace as though he were suffering from acute toothache. 'To be honest with you, this is beyond me, Mr Holmes. I do hope you can see your way to shedding some light on the matter.'

'Delighted to, Hardcastle,' said Holmes, throwing me a sidelong glance. 'You know I'm always happy to assist the official force whenever I am able.'

The policeman beamed and his body visibly relaxed. 'That's wonderful,' he said. 'I have a cab waiting. If you'd be so good, we can go round to the British Museum now. Sir Charles Pargetter, the Curator of the Egyptology section, can explain to you all about this blasted papyrus.'

'Excellent,' cried Holmes, flinging off his dressing gown. 'Are you game, Watson?'

'Certainly.'

'Then, my dear fellow, collect your coat, hat, and stick and we shall accompany our friend here to the British Museum!'

SIR CHARLES DISCOURSES

'Of course, I was once an habitué of this noble building. When I first arrived in London, making my way in the world, I had rooms round in Montague Street, and I often came here to study in the reading room, which also had the additional benefits of being warm and free.' So announced Sherlock Holmes as, together with Inspector Hardcastle, we passed through the great gates of the museum and approached the eight massive ionic columns which stand, as sentinels, before its entrance.

Once inside, Hardcastle took the lead and led us towards the office of Sir Charles Pargetter. To reach it, we had to pass beyond the public area of the museum. At this point, a heavily-moustached member of the security staff checked the policeman's credentials thoroughly before allowing us to progress further. We then moved down a series of hushed, narrow, dimly-lighted corridors until, at last, we came to a door which bore the name of the man whom we were there to meet.

Hardcastle knocked loudly. There was a brief pause, and then a strident voice, tinged with irritation, called out, 'Enter.'

We found ourselves in a bright, airy room with one large curtainless window which looked out on the north-west wing of the museum. The room itself was crammed with bookcases, all overflowing, and the floor was littered with various documents and note-books. Sir Charles was standing behind a large oak desk, leaning forward, scrutinising an ancient map through a magnifying glass. He failed to look up at our entrance, but continued to gaze, mesmerised, at the map.

With deliberation, Holmes slammed the door shut. This broke the man's concentration and, uttering a grunt of irritation, he glanced up at us. He was a small man, Pickwickian in appearance, with bright blue eyes shining behind a pair of wire-framed spectacles. He was bald-headed, but the hair at the side of his head, sandy in colour but peppered with grey, stuck out in confusion as though it were bursting free of his scalp.

'Ah, Inspector Horncastle,' he said, his eyes narrowing as he took in his other two visitors.

'Hardcastle, sir,' corrected the Inspector.

'Quite.' Sir Charles waved his magnifying glass in our direction. 'Don't tell me you have apprehended the culprits at last?'

Hardcastle, who was unable to catch the tinge of irony in this remark, looked somewhat dismayed. 'No, sir. This is Mr Sherlock Holmes and his associate, Doctor Watson.'

At the mention of my friend's name, Sir Charles threw down the magnifying glass, stepped from behind the desk, and grasped Holmes' hand warmly. 'Ah, Sherlock Holmes. You have come to our aid, I hope.'

'I will do all I can.'

Sir Charles nodded thoughtfully as he shook my hand also. 'Indeed, it is all that one can do in life. We are placed upon this Earth to perform a series of tasks, whatever they may be, lowly or exalted, and it is incumbent upon us all to perform them to the very best of our ability. Eh, Inspector?'

Hardcastle nodded and shifted his feet. He had no time for such philosophical niceties; he was keen to get on with the business in hand. 'Mr Holmes is here to find out more about the robbery,' he said bluntly.

'Indeed. How may I help?'

'I need to know more of the nature of the stolen document before I can construct any theories which could form a basis for action,' said Holmes.

'I understand. Very well, find a seat gentlemen... you may have to move some of my papers to do so. That's right. Good. Oh dear, there doesn't seem to be a chair for you, Inspector.'

'I'm quite happy to stand, sir,' came the muted reply.

Now seated behind his desk, the little man was almost dwarfed by it. He removed his spectacles and cleaned them with an enormous blue handkerchief.

'You must realise, gentlemen,' he said, 'I am still in mourning for the loss of the papyrus. It was quite unique. Ah, but let me begin at the beginning.' He replaced his glasses and leaned back in his chair. 'In 1871, two British archaeologists, Sir George Faversham and Sir Alistair Andrews, discovered a tomb in Upper Egypt containing forty mummies. They lay scattered and in varying states of decay. Some, which had been moved from other tombs, were hidden down a secret vertical passageway. One mummy, in a makeshift sarcophagus, was discovered in a cunning shaft running at right angles to this passageway. Protection against grave robbers, you understand. This, it was discovered, was the mummy of Queen Henntawy.

'She was only twenty-one or two when she died. We know that she was the wife of Pinneedjem I, the first king of the Twenty-first Dynasty. He was served by the high priest Setaph, who dabbled in the Black Arts and was indeed said to be a reincarnation of Osiris, God of the Dead. The story goes that Pinneedjem was so distraught by the death of his young wife that he begged Setaph to work his magic and bring her back to life. You must realise that the Ancient Egyptians believed in the afterlife. Once death had overtaken them, they had to pass through the Underworld, a dark and dangerous region before they reached final bliss.'

'In The Field of Reeds.'

'Indeed, Mr Holmes, the equivalent of our heaven. The voyage to the afterlife was aided by the inclusion in the tomb of certain artefacts and necessities useful for the journey and for the "life" on the other side. Included with these items was the Scroll of the Dead, sheets of papyrus covered with magical texts and accompanying vignettes – spells, if you like – to help the dead pass through the dangers of the Underworld and reach The Field of Reeds safely.

'Now, Pinneedjem did not want Henntawy to undertake that particular journey. He wanted her alive again: living and breathing, with him to enjoy the pleasures of this life. So he implored, and no doubt threatened, Setaph to create a new Scroll of the Dead containing spells that would, in effect, conquer death.' Here Sir Toby paused and afforded himself a smile. 'Not an easy task for any man. However, as I intimated previously, Setaph dabbled in the Black Arts and supposedly had Osiris on his side, so he was able to meet the demands made upon him. However, his Scroll of the Dead was never used, for when it was discovered by the Gods that he had learned the secret of everlasting life they forbade him to use it. He was commanded to destroy the Scroll, but instead he hid it, hoping no doubt to use it himself one day. Unfortunately for Setaph, death overtook him before he was able to avail himself of its powers. On his instructions, the temple priests buried him in a secret location with all his artefacts and papers, including the Scroll. Setaph was a cunning man and he fully believed that he had discovered the magic process that would transcend death. Although he had been forbidden by the Gods to use it, he was not going to let his fantastic secret die with him. So he left a remarkable trail for someone with the same ingenious imagination as himself to follow, to discover his own secret tomb which contains the Scroll of the Dead. He recorded details of its whereabouts on a papyrus secreted on the mummified body of his Queen, Henntawy.

'Setaph's Scroll of the Dead is one of the most sought after Egyptian relics of all. No one has seen it in modern times, but there is evidence from the ancient world that it exists.'

'So this was not the document that was stolen?' I asked.

Sir Charles shook his head. 'When Henntawy's sarcophagus was opened, it was found that her mummy was in a remarkable state of preservation and, secreted amongst the folds of the bandages, there was a papyrus. It was this that the thieves made away with last week.'

'What are the contents of the papyrus?' asked Holmes, whose face had remained immobile during Sir Charles' discourse.

'It is a strange document written in a peculiar cipher – Setaph's own code. The hieroglyphics are perversions of those used at the period of the Twenty-first Dynasty and there are also additions of Setaph's own invention. What we do know is that it was written by Setaph himself. He signed it and marked it with his personal insignia: a half-scarab. This papyrus would seem to give directions to the location of his own tomb.'

'It is a kind of map, then?' I asked

Sir Charles smiled at me. 'In simple terms, Doctor, yes. It is clear that there are passages relating to Setaph's philosophy and some dedications of allegiance to Pinneedjem and Henntawy. References to Osiris are also made, but the whole remains a mystery...'

'Including the location of Setaph's tomb,' said Holmes.

'Yes.'

'So this could very well be the motive for stealing the document: to discover the hidden burial place.'

Sir Charles gave a shrug of the shoulder. 'A fanciful theft if it was. Both the archaeologists who discovered the papyrus were unable to make any real sense of it and since then, from time to time, it has been examined by qualified men, Egyptologists of note, who thought they had the key.'

'When was it last scrutinised in such a way?'

'Not for some time, I think. Ten years possibly. I could find out if you consider it to be important.'

'It may be,' said Holmes, thoughtfully. 'Let us suppose for a moment that those responsible for the theft of the papyrus are able to interpret the messages within it, break the code of the map and, therefore, seek out the tomb of Setaph. What would they gain for their trouble?'

'Very little in material wealth. Setaph was, after all, only a high priest. There will be a few gold items, various altar relics and ornaments, but little else in worldly goods.' Here Sir Charles paused and, leaning over the desk, he lowered his voice almost to a whisper. 'There will, of course,' he said, 'be Setaph's magical Scroll of the Dead.'

Three

THE SCENES OF THE CRIMES

'We were only able to keep the Egyptian gallery closed for one day after the crime on the pretext of auditing part of the collection; any longer and I'm sure the newspaper reporters would have sniffed something in the wind.'

Sir Charles Pargetter was explaining this point as we stood on the threshold of the Egyptian gallery where some half a dozen visitors were strolling around, peering at the various exhibits. The room was divided into three sections, comprising a series of glass exhibition cases, several containing the brown and ragged bodies of ancient mummies, as well as those which displayed many beautiful carved objects and precious artefacts from that remarkable civilisation which flourished at the dawn of time. High above us, running in a frieze around the wall and softly illuminated by the new electric lighting, was a series of scenes from Ancient Egyptian life.

'What was your concern about the story of the theft being printed in the newspapers?' I asked.

'No museum likes to admit that it has lost one of its treasures, Doctor.

It would deter potential benefactors, and any story like that would act as an advertisement to the criminal fraternity: come to the British Museum and steal – it is so easy.'

'It was also in *our* best interests, as I explained,' added the Scotland Yarder.

'How did the men enter, Hardcastle?'

In response to my friend's query, the policeman pointed at the roof of the chamber. Set into the curved ceiling were three large rectangular skylights which provided the main illumination of the room.

'They forced one of them open and dropped down on a rope, and returned by the same route. On leaving, they carelessly dropped their rope and we found it coiled on the floor over by Henntawy's case.'

Holmes peered up at the skylights and then back at Sir Charles. 'Where is the case?'

'This way gentlemen, please,' replied the Egyptologist, leading us down the central aisle and stopping mid-way, before a glass case which was situated on its own. 'Queen Henntawy,' he announced with a grand gesture.

I felt an uneasy prickle at the back of my neck as I gazed down on the remains of this young woman who had been alive more than 3000 years ago. The heavily-painted face was in a fantastic state of preservation, appearing mask-like with false ebony eyes placed in the empty sockets, locked in a dark, vacant stare. A heavy Medusa-like wig spilled out around her shrunken head. The length of her body was covered in rotting brown bandages.

'Isn't she beautiful?' said Sir Charles, beaming.

'I must admit,' said Hardcastle seriously, 'she's not exactly my idea of a beauty.'

Holmes crouched down and slowly circled the case, stopping from time to time with his nose against the glass to scrutinise the mummy within. At length he rose and pointed to a particularly ragged part of the body by the thigh. 'Is this where the papyrus rested?'

Sir Charles' mouth opened in surprise. 'Why, yes, Mr Holmes. How very astute of you.'

'It is clear that those tears are fairly recent – the material shows traces of whiteness here – and it is only the glass on this side of the case that you have had to replace. The putty is quite fresh. Obviously our expert knew exactly where to look.'

'Presumably,' I observed quietly, 'it was the sound of the breaking glass that alerted the security guard, and he was murdered when he came to investigate.'

Sir Charles shook his head gravely. 'Oh no, Doctor. He was killed in his office.'

'What!' I exclaimed, glancing at Holmes, who was equally shocked.

'Why did you not tell me about this, Hardcastle?' enquired my friend sharply.

The Scotland Yarder hesitated, bracing himself for Holmes' wrath. 'Well,' he stammered, his face blanching, 'I really didn't consider it an important feature of the crime.'

Holmes closed his eyes in disgust and gave a derisory snort. 'It not only provides us with further information concerning the perpetrators of the theft, it also indicates the means by which it was committed.'

We all fell silent at this declaration, until Sir Charles, eyes wide behind his spectacles, said, 'Well, this is a most remarkable claim. Pray do expound.'

'I should first like to examine the security guard's office, if I may.'

'Certainly,' said Sir Charles. 'Follow me.'

The room in question was a small, cluttered chamber filled by a stout wooden table on which stood a gas ring, a couple of mugs, and various items of tea-making equipment. As we entered, a chubby young man, rubicund of visage, who was sitting back in a battered old carver chair with his feet on the table, reading *The Racing Gazette*, jumped to his feet and stood crookedly to attention.

'Sorry, Sir Charles,' he croaked in a gentle Cockney accent, the pouches of his rosy cheeks reverberating nervously at the shock of our sudden entrance. 'I didn't know you was comin', Sir. I'm on my tea-break now.' Realising the newspaper was still in his hand, he quickly crumpled it up and attempted to hide it behind his back.

The Egyptologist gave a thin smile. 'That's all right, Jenkins. I'm not checking up on my staff today. These gentlemen are investigating the theft of Henntawy's papyrus and Daventry's murder, and they wish to examine the room where he died.' At this point he broke off and turned to Holmes. 'Jenkins is the regular day guard for this wing of the museum,' he explained. 'We haven't as yet got round to replacing Daventry. His duties are being shared by the other night staff at present.'

Holmes nodded and, stepping forward, addressed the young guard. 'You found the body, Jenkins?'

'Er, yes, sir. On Saturday mornin'. I... I came on at eight in the mornin' as usual. At first everything seemed as right as pie... until I got in here. I found him there, on the rug.' He pointed and we all gazed at the floor space where, clearly, a rug had been laid. The faint rectangular outline was visible against the dark brown of the scuffed floorboards. 'There wasn't much blood – just a dark spot on the side of his head.' The chubby cheeks paled momentarily and then the young man afforded himself a little affectionate grin. 'Old Sammy – that's Mr Daventry, like – old Sammy, he was a nice bloke. Him an' me would often have a cuppa and a natter together in the mornin' before he went off to his kip.'

'You would discuss racing, perhaps? Choose the best bets for the day?' said Holmes.

Nervously, Jenkins crumpled the paper behind his back and glanced at Sir Charles. 'Ye– Yes, sir.'

'Don't be nervous,' continued Holmes. 'Gambling is not against the law, despite it being a somewhat reckless pursuit. Indeed, I have a friend who fritters a fair deal of his income away on the fickleness of the turf.'

'Well, it is true that we liked a flutter. We'd often have a bet together. I have a wife and a young 'un on the way so I daren't risk much, but old Sammy...'

'He was a big gambler.'

'Yes, sir.'

'And a big loser.'

The brown eyes fixed in that apple-red face dimmed and shifted once more to Sir Charles.

Holmes carried on relentlessly. 'In fact, Jenkins, I would suspect that your friend was up to his eyes in debt. Am I correct?'

Jenkins faltered once more.

'Tell the truth, Jenkins,' prompted Sir Charles as the guard stared dumbly at his feet. 'Whatever Daventry did, it is no reflection on you.'

'Well,' said Jenkins, clearing his throat and coughing nervously as he began, 'if the truth be known, old Sammy was in quite deep with the money lenders. It frightened me what he told me about their threats to him if he didn't pay up. He always laughed it off, sayin' that somethin' would always turn up.'

'And it did,' said Holmes, grimly.

'Just a minute, Mr Holmes. You're not suggesting that his murder was committed by money-lender's thugs, are you?' asked Hardcastle, a note of incredulity in his voice.

Holmes gave a shake of the head. 'Tell me, Jenkins, where did Daventry keep his private belongings?'

'In his locker, sir. We each have one.' He pointed to the corner of the room where two tall rusty metal lockers leaned drunkenly against each other.

Holmes crossed to them. 'Which was Daventry's?'

Jenkins pointed again.

Holmes turned the handle. 'It's locked. Has this been opened since the murder?' He addressed the question to Hardcastle and all heads turned in his direction.

The policeman shrugged with as much nonchalance as his obvious bewilderment and unease would allow. 'We haven't touched it at all. It's not really relevant to the theft... or the murder.'

'Where is the key?' snapped Holmes.

'I expect it'll be down at the Yard with the rest of Daventry's effects.'

'Hah!' Holmes snarled, and fumbled for a moment in his waistcoat pocket, before producing a small penknife. 'In the absence of a key, this makeshift burgling kit will have to suffice.'

So saying, he inserted the small blade into the gap between the door and the side of the locker and applied some pressure on the lock. 'A little knowledge... and a great deal more brute force... should win the day,' he grunted as he worked at his task.

After less than a minute, there was a reverberating clang and the locker door sprang open. '*Voilà!*' cried my friend.

'What is all this, Mr Holmes?' cried Hardcastle warily, unable to contain his bewilderment. 'What tricks are you playing now?'

'No tricks, I assure you, Inspector – and I will explain everything in just a moment.'

Holmes began rummaging around in the locker. Moments later he emitted a cry of triumph as he extricated a small brown parcel from its recesses. 'Here,' he cried, throwing it to Jenkins. 'Unwrap that, my boy, and feast your eyes on the contents.'

On receiving a nod of approval from Sir Charles, Jenkins set about his appointed task. With nervous fingers he began to pare away the brown wrapping, slowly at first and then with feverish excitement as the last layer was exposed. Finally, the contents of the parcel were revealed: a large brown leather purse. Holmes took it from the lad and spilled out the contents on to the table. An irregular pyramid of bright yellow coins glittered before us.

'Blimey!' cried Jenkins. 'There's a fortune here.'

'Some would say so, lad.' Holmes ran his long fingers through the pile, scooped up a few of the coins, and held them before the astonished faces of Sir Charles and Hardcastle. 'There will be a hundred guineas here. Not bad for a night's work. That's if Daventry had lived to reap the benefit from his ill-gotten gains.'

'Ill-gotten?' I said.

'Yes. This is the fee our friend Daventry was paid to admit the thieves to the museum and then to turn a blind eye while they went about their business.'

'You mean to say he was in league with the criminals?' gasped Sir Charles.

'In a manner of speaking. A fellow's debts have a habit of becoming well-known in certain circles. Those with a need to know can easily find out these things. In such circumstances, there is little difficulty in bribing a man who is desperate for money.'

'Bribing?'

'Yes, Inspector.' Holmes pointed to the pile of sovereigns. 'Daventry was offered this princely sum to aid in the theft of the Henntawy papyrus.'

'So you're saying they just walked in, took the papyrus, and walked out again, while Daventry held the door for them.'

'Yes, in a manner of speaking. Very civilised, eh?'

'But what about the rope and the footprints?'

'False clues to lead you astray. The method of entry and exit was rather too obviously presented to us. We were being led by the nose to believe that the crimes had been perpetrated by two experienced but common burglars. Think, man. How did they get up on the roof in the first place? Surely their presence there would have attracted the attention of other officers?' Holmes glanced at Sir Charles for confirmation of this and received a hesitant nod of agreement. 'Have your men been on the roof to check these things out, Hardcastle?'

'I sent a couple of constables up there. But they found nothing.'

'You did not go up yourself?'

'Why, no. I did not think there would be any point.' The inspector looked perplexed.

'In this instance you were correct. You would have found nothing there. The skylights can be opened from inside by using one of the long window poles designed for the purpose. I observed two in the Egyptology room. Then it is a simple task to drop a coil of rope under one such open skylight and leave a few false muddy footprints to create the impression that two men had dropped from the heavens, snatched a precious document, and ascended like dark angels.'

'If this is so, why go to all the bother?'

Holmes smiled. 'To muddy the waters – to help disguise the identity of the intruders. What we have here, gentlemen, is not a simple crime but the cunning theft of an object of antiquity with a cold-blooded murder as merely an unfortunate side-issue. The preposterous clues of the rope and the footprints were unnecessary if the only object of the operation was to steal the papyrus. But they were necessary to the perpetrators – they were part of their game, to enhance the excitement of the venture and to ridicule the authorities. I am convinced that these fellows fully intended to shoot the security guard before they set foot in the building. The murder was more or less gratuitous, adding an extra *frisson* of pleasure to their nocturnal exploits.'

'If what you say is true, then we are dealing with madmen,' retorted Sir Charles.

'To some extent, I agree with you. What normal felons would leave behind their bribe of a hundred guineas, when they had murdered its recipient? As our antagonists saw it, they were merely carrying out the perverted rules of their contract with Daventry – paying for services rendered. It did not matter whether the fellow was dead or not. They had honoured their agreement. Rich men, then, and indeed, tainted with madness.'

Before Sir Charles could respond, Hardcastle thrust an indignant finger towards my friend's face. 'This is mere guesswork,' he retorted.

Holmes shook his head. 'Consider the evidence,' he replied softly. 'First: the obvious way in which clues were left to indicate the means of entry. It was too simplistic. The operation was carried out with such panache that these clues were preserved like clumsy signs in a children's game. To an experienced investigator like myself, it is clear that they were planted. This was in order to further confuse the issues. A successful ruse, for three days later you are no wiser as to the culprits or the motive. Secondly: the object of the crime, the theft of an obscure papyrus, can really only be of interest to specialists, individuals – strange individuals – who desire the item desperately, for whatever purpose, and are prepared to kill for it. Thirdly: the fact that the security guard was shot in his own office indicates that in some way he was implicated in the crime. The only real need to kill him would arise if he had surprised the intruders while they were about their nefarious task. In that case there would have been a struggle resulting in a rather messy killing, which is not our villains' style at all. Remember there was no struggle and only one bullet in the gun. Daventry died because he trusted the man who had bribed him. He was like a lamb to the slaughter: the killer, most likely, just came up to the guard, little gun in hand, and fired so...'

Holmes demonstrated by placing two fingers at Jenkins's temples. The young man groaned and dropped into his chair.

'Quite clearly, Daventry was "in" on the job, and that would make just one accomplice too many in this affair. I believe this to be the work of a brilliant but sadistic mind – someone who is obsessed and desperate enough to want the papyrus for himself. It will not be passed on to others. Why else would he kill a foolish and impoverished security guard? In order that there was no possibility, however remote, that anyone would be able to trace him. Our villain is a cunning and dangerous creature.'

'You have reverted to the singular, Mr Holmes. I thought you said there were two of them involved in this business,' said Hardcastle smoothly.

'I do not deny that there were two malefactors who perpetrated this audacious crime, but the conception and the purpose...' He paused and turned his steely gaze on the inspector. 'There is but one brain behind this affair and it is as perverted as it is clever.'

'Who is this mastermind, then?' asked Hardcastle. 'You cannot blame Professor Moriarty this time.'

Holmes eyed the police inspector coldly. 'One of your more astute observations, Hardcastle. Whoever we are dealing with has something of the professor's ingenuity, daring and, I am afraid, cold-bloodedness. A man of great intelligence and a man to fear.'

Four

An Unexpected Event

'The heavily notated racing calendar on the wall and the discarded copies of *The Racing Gazette* on the table informed me that Jenkins and Daventry were betting men and, as you well know, Watson, gambling men are rarely in pocket.'

I nodded with a smile.

My friend struck a match and applied it to his pipe. For a brief moment, dense grey clouds obliterated his face. It was now some hours since we had left the British Museum and we were back once more in our Baker Street rooms. The gas mantles had just been lit as the day began to fade. Holmes, wrapped in his blue dressing gown, was pleased with himself and in a communicative mood. 'I do not think,' said he, throwing his match to the back of the grate, 'that it will be many days before this case is wrapped up.'

'But there are so many unanswered questions.'

'I can answer them.'

'Really,' I said gruffly, trying to restrain the note of incredulity in my voice.

'There is no great mystery, Watson.'

'Then who is the culprit? Who is the thief?'

Holmes beamed. 'Consider the problem objectively and logically. A document has been stolen. Other, more valuable artefacts were ignored in favour of this crumbling and indecipherable papyrus. Therefore, the scroll was purloined for its singular contents rather than for its intrinsic value.'

'Well, yes, I can see that; but, really, all it contained was some obscure writings about the location of Setaph's tomb.'

'And his Scroll of the Dead.'

'But what use is that? Experts have tried to solve the riddle and discover the whereabouts of this Scroll of the Dead and failed. What chance has anyone else?'

Sherlock Holmes emitted a faint groan. 'Watson, Watson,' he said with some passion, 'extend the boundaries of thought. Don't always remain with the possible or the probable. Consider also the unlikely, the improbable – and the obvious.'

'The obvious,' I echoed, shaking my head. 'I'm afraid you have lost me.'

'The Henntawy papyrus contains a code. A code is merely a means of presenting information in a hidden form. In order to avail yourself of this information, what do you need?'

'The key.'

'Exactly. As we have been told, Setaph was a shrewd and cunning man. He was fully aware of the dangers of common grave robbers ransacking Henntawy's tomb and finding the papyrus giving details of his own resting place and the location of his magic Scroll. So, in order to protect his secret and provide a puzzle that only the inspired seeker of life beyond death could solve, he created his own code. But for that code there had to be a key and he placed the key, probably on another simple document, elsewhere, ready to be discovered by the chosen one – the special one who is able to utilise his "secrets of immortality".'

'And you think that our thief has come into possession of the key to Setaph's message?'

'I do; and therefore this papyrus which has been languishing in the British Museum for years now assumes great importance to him. It is essential that he possess it.'

'I suppose all this is possible.'

'Aha, now you have moved your thinking beyond the limitations of the available data.'

'Perhaps,' I said, 'but I still do not know how such a key could be obtained.'

'I frequently read of Egyptian antiquities turning up in trinket shops in the city. Smuggled goods that are bought and sold by unscrupulous dealers, most of whom would not be able to tell Egyptian icons from those of the Aztec civilisation. It is a trade in ancient curiosities which has existed for centuries.'

'And so you think some sort of document containing the key to Henntawy's scroll found its way into one of these shops you mention, and was picked up by someone who knew its real value?'

He nodded. 'It is a possibility. One with which we can play to see where it leads us.'

'It seems a somewhat fantastic conclusion.'

'Nonsense: it fits all known facts. If our thief is the man I take him to be he will have employed agents to keep a watch on such places in case anything juicy turned up... anything bearing Setaph's mark: the half scarab.'

'Can you be sure?'

'Not yet; but my supposition is not only possible, but most probable.'

'So the Scroll of the Dead is the real prize.'

'Bravo, Watson.'

'But how can this fellow sell it on the open market without giving the game away as to how it came into his possession?'

Holmes eyed me seriously, his features set in a firm and concentrated expression. 'He does not mean to sell it. He means to use it.'

There was a moment's pause while the import of Holmes' remark sank in; and then the hairs on the back of my neck bristled. 'You mean he believes that this Scroll will give him power over death?'

'Yes.'

'Why, the man must be insane.'

'In all probability he is.'

'Good grief! You speak as though you know his identity.'

'I do.'

'You do!' I cried in utter astonishment.

Holmes puffed on his pipe, eyeing me with some amusement.

'Holmes,' I said, 'don't be so infuriating. Who is he?'

'Sebastian Melmoth.'

'What?'

'You remember him?'

'Of course I remember him. But surely you cannot think that he, strange and immoral though he obviously is, would stoop to theft and murder?'

'With the kind of obsession he harbours, I am sure there is nothing to which he would not stoop. Remember the blond hair I extracted from the Derringer trigger guard and the smell on the weapon of that pungent cologne? The same, I am sure, that the fellow was doused in when he came here. You see, Watson, since his macabre declarations in this room about a year ago, I have kept my eye on that malevolent young man.'

'How?'

'Through the gossip columns and through my own agency. I know that he has been searching for something – something he desires desperately. No doubt because of his researches into death, he would for some time have known of Setaph's coded papyrus lodged in the British

Museum and has been investigating the likelihood of obtaining a key document in order to break the code and expose its precious secret. Now I believe he has that key.'

'If what you say is true, then he will be off to Egypt without delay in an attempt to get his hands on the Scroll of the Dead.'

Holmes gave a thin smile. 'That is if he has managed to break the code and thereby solve the riddle of the scroll. Having the key is one thing – but using it is another. Such matters require knowledge and understanding of the the Ancient Egyptian mind and civilisation.'

'What do you intend to do?'

'We shall call on Mr Melmoth first thing in the morning, and I will confront him with what I know. His reactions will be most interesting to observe. It is a meeting I shall relish.'

It was a bright May morning, with a pale blue sky and thin, ragged clouds scudding across the heavens, as Holmes and I approached Sebastian Melmoth's town house in Curzon Street. I was extremely apprehensive about our visit on two counts. Firstly, it seemed to me that there was just too much supposition in Holmes' theory to render it certain and I feared that he might, for the first time in his life, be making a very big mistake. Secondly, I did not relish placing myself in the company of Melmoth again; I felt rather like a child frightened of the dark – knowing that the fear is irrational and yet that it is there and all too real.

Holmes pulled the bell and we heard it ring in the far reaches of the house. Presently the door was opened by a saturnine young man, with dark, baleful eyes and an air of intimidating arrogance, whom I took, wrongly as it turned out, to be Melmoth's manservant. Holmes extracted a calling card from his waistcoat pocket and presented it to the young man without a word.

The fellow examined it sardonically, even turning it over to discover if there was anything on the reverse side, and then, leaning indolently against the door frame, he raised his eyebrows in a facetious manner. 'Yes, what is it?' he asked, waving Holmes' card carelessly.

'Please inform Mr Melmoth that I wish to see him on urgent business,' said Holmes sharply.

For a moment there was the ghost of a smile on those swarthy and arrogant features. 'If you want to see Sebastian urgently, then I suggest you "go look for him in the other place",' he said, and this time the red lips did stretch back into a smile, revealing a thin line of white teeth.

Holmes frowned. 'I will not be deterred, sir,' he said with some warmth.

'I am afraid you will. Apparently, you have not heard the sad news,' said the young man casually, apparently brushing some invisible speck of dust from his sleeve. 'I regret to inform you that Mr Sebastian Melmoth is dead.'

Five

FURTHER TWISTS

Never in all the years that I have known Sherlock Holmes did I see him look more shocked and dismayed than he did on hearing that Sebastian Melmoth was dead. For a moment he remained motionless, as though struck dumb by the import of this news – news which threw all his deductions and plans into complete disarray.

'When did it happen?' I asked the youth, partly out of curiosity and partly in an attempt to cover up my friend's hesitancy.

'The day before yesterday,' came the languid reply. 'Seb was involved in a shooting accident on my father's estate in Norfolk.'

'Your father...?'

'...is Lord Felshaw.'

'A shooting accident, you say?' prompted Holmes, regaining some of his composure.

The youth nodded. 'Yes. Sad business,' he replied, without any emotion in his voice. 'We were out shooting with Briggs, one of our keepers, when Sebastian lost us for a while in the undergrowth. We heard a shot and found him dead.'

'What happened?'

He gave a light shrug of the shoulders. 'His gun must have gone off accidentally. A rather messy business really.'

'You don't seem to have been upset by the incident,' I remarked tersely, the fellow's easy arrogance beginning to rankle.

'We all die at some time. Seb, of all people, was probably quite happy to try it out. The final great experiment, y'know.' A shadow of a sly grin passed over his sharp features and then he paused and breathed deeply as though taking the air. 'Now, gentlemen, if you will excuse me, the morning is far too chilly to allow one to stand on the doorstep indulging in idle chatter. The funeral ceremony is tomorrow and I have arrangements to make.' Just before closing the door on us, he added pointedly: 'It will be a very private affair. Attendance is by invitation only.'

Holmes remained taciturn and silent as we made our way back to Baker Street. His gloomy features told of the pain and indignity that he felt at being proved so wrong in his deductions. As we turned into Baker Street once more, I attempted some words of consolation.

He gave a sharp intake of breath before replying. 'Save your sympathies, Watson. Melmoth's demise does not alter the facts. He was the one who murdered Daventry and stole the papyrus from the museum.'

'How on earth can you prove it now?'

He tapped his forehead. 'It is here, but not yet engendered.'

Smiling briefly, he took my arm and led me towards our door. 'There is more in this business than we can yet see, but I am convinced that I am on the right track. Events will evolve which will provide us with more light.'

There was a further surprise for us when we entered our sitting-room. We had a client awaiting our return. A young, fresh-faced woman attired in a fashionable green velvet dress rose from the seat by the fire to greet us. She was tall and slender, with stylishly-dressed, copper-coloured hair, and a pair of challenging brown eyes. 'Mr Holmes?' she said, gazing uncertainly from one to the other.

'I am he,' replied Holmes, pulling off his coat and draping it over the wooden chair by his work bench. 'And this is my friend and colleague, Doctor Watson, Miss...?'

'Andrews – Catriona Andrews.' She spoke clearly and confidently and yet there was a certain nervousness about her demeanour. It was not, I surmised, a natural diffidence, but one brought about by worry and concern.

'Resume your seat, Miss Andrews. Would you care for some refreshment? Tea perhaps?'

The young woman shook her head with determination. 'No, no, nothing thank you. I am anxious to explain why I am here.'

Holmes threw himself down in his chair and with a broad gesture bade me to take a seat also. 'My colleague and I are all attention. Please take your time and relay your problem clearly and in full detail.' So saying he slumped back and closed his eyes.

Our visitor leaned forward in her chair and began her narrative. She spoke in clear, well-modulated tones which contained only a faint trace of her Scottish ancestry. 'As I have already told you, I am Catriona Andrews: the daughter of Sir Alistair Andrews.'

'The archaeologist?' I cried.

'Yes.' At this point our visitor faltered, her head drooped, and she retrieved a handkerchief from her reticule to dab her moist eyes. 'My father... my father has disappeared.'

Holmes, who did not seem at all surprised at this sudden revelation, nodded his head in understanding without even opening his eyes. 'Pray begin at the beginning, Miss Andrews,' he said softly.

The brave young woman gave a shake of the shoulders, stuffed the handkerchief back into her reticule, and began again. 'My mother died shortly after my birth, and so the full responsibility for my upbringing fell to my father. That is perhaps why I feel closer to my father than do most daughters. We live together in a comfortable villa in St John's Wood. I act as his assistant – helping him in his work, typing his papers, co-ordinating the catalogue of his vast collection of relics which he has accumulated from his various expeditions.

'Everything was fine between us until just recently, when he began behaving oddly – shunning most visitors and spending more and more of his time locked up in his study. About a week ago he began taking his meals in there alone. He would also go out late at night and not return until it was almost morning. When I asked him about these nocturnal expeditions, he told me sharply that it was his private business.' She shook her head sadly. 'It was so very unlike my father – we always shared so much, and now he was shutting me out. You can imagine how concerned and hurt I was by his behaviour. It was as though he had become another person.

'And then yesterday he did not return at all. His bed had not been slept in and there was no note to indicate where he might have gone. I was beside myself with worry. I was about to contact the police when this letter arrived by the four o'clock delivery.' She passed me a crumpled sheet of paper on which was written the following message:

Dear C

I shall be away for some time.

Forgive me for not informing you of my

absence, but, believe me, I have my reasons.

Do not worry about me: I am perfectly safe

and well, but under no circumstances contact

the authorities about my disappearance. I will
explain all when I return.

All my love

'What is this design?' I asked, pointing to a scribbled drawing which took the place of a signature.

'I do not know how well you know your Egyptology, Doctor Watson, but it is Thoth, the ibis-headed scribe of the Gods. That is my father's special signature. He used it when he wrote me playful notes when I was very young. It is a kind of secret between us. That is why I know that the note is genuine.'

'Signatures can be learned, however obscure,' observed Holmes. 'There is no doubt about the handwriting?'

'None whatsoever. I am sure this note came from my father.'

'Miss Andrews, you said that your father shunned most visitors...' She nodded.

'But not all?'

'No. There was one man who called on two occasions who was quickly ushered into his room.'

'You knew this man?'

'No. I had never seen him before. I do not even know his name.'

'Describe him please.'

'He was young. About thirty, I should say. Well dressed in a rather flamboyant manner. He was very pale and had long blond hair.'

'Why Holmes...' I cried, recognising this description of Sebastian Melmoth.

My friend put his fingers to his lips. 'Fascinating, isn't it, Watson? Now, Miss Andrews, allow me to examine the note.'

Holmes took the sheet of cream paper from her outstretched hand and scrutinised it with his lens. 'Hmm. The writing is crabbed and erratic –

obviously written under some duress. The pen splutters some five times, indicating that the message did not spring freely from the writer's mind but was dictated to him.' He held the paper to the window. 'Is this your own notepaper, Miss Andrews?'

'No. My father always insists on white.'

'It is a quality paper, probably costing fourpence a sheet, leading one to suppose that our kidnappers are quite wealthy.'

'Kidnappers!' Both Miss Andrews and I burst out with the same exclamation simultaneously.

Holmes smiled. 'Indeed. All the evidence – slim though it is – leads me to the inevitable conclusion that your father has been kidnapped.'

At times Holmes was so concerned with displaying his talents for deduction that he gave little thought to the effect his revelations would have on those he was addressing. Miss Andrews, her face drained of colour, gripped the arms of her chair and leant forward towards my friend. There was, however, a steady gleam in her eye that clearly showed her reserve and courage. When she spoke, her voice was clear and controlled, but edged with suppressed anger. 'You cannot mean it, Mr Holmes. Who would want to kidnap my father? And why? Besides, there has been no ransom note. Surely you are mistaken.'

'I fear not. However, I do not believe that your father's life is in danger for the present.'

I placed a comforting hand on the young lady's shoulder and frowned at my friend. 'Holmes,' I said sharply, 'stop talking in riddles. Miss Andrews has a right to have a clear explanation from you.'

'Of course,' he replied, with little conviction.

'If her father has been abducted, why has there been no communication from the kidnappers?'

'Because they have what they want already: not money, but Sir Alistair's specialist knowledge.'

'I'm sorry, Mr Holmes, but I am completely baffled by all this. Please explain things to me clearly.'

'I cannot take you fully into my confidence just yet, Miss Andrews, but I can assure you that...'

But Holmes could get no further with his assurances. A sudden change had come over our visitor. She rose to her feet, her whole frame bristling with indignation, and halted Holmes in mid-sentence with a violent wave of her hand. 'That is not good enough, sir,' she cried vehemently, her eyes sparking fire and the colour rising in her cheeks. 'If you know something concerning my father's disappearance, it is your duty to tell me. I am no delicate flower unable to take bad news — whatever it may be. I am determined and responsible. I have accompanied my father on many of his digs and endured conditions and undergone tasks which would have made many men tremble. You may be in control of your world, Mr Holmes, but do not make the mistake of thinking that all women are feeble, brainless little things who must be protected from the cruel blows of life. They are not. I can assure you that *I* am certainly not. I will not be patronised or placated. Therefore, I demand that you tell me all you know.'

This certainly was a day to challenge Sherlock Holmes. His jaw muscles tightened and there was a momentary flicker of anger in his eyes; then, as though containing his irritation, he stretched his legs out and leaned back in the chair, chuckling gently to himself. 'How can I resist such an entreaty, eh, Watson?' It was an uneasy response, and he had not quite managed to capture the air of nonchalance that he had intended.

I did not reply; in fact, I deliberately averted my gaze from both Holmes and the young woman. I did not want to become involved in this brittle *tête-à-tête*. It did my heart good to have a woman put my friend in his place. My Mary often said that, despite all his skills as a reasoner, Holmes had a most faulty understanding of the female psyche and tended to treat all women in the same manner. Miss Andrews was proving him wrong.

'Well, sir, I am waiting...'

Holmes gave a sigh of resignation. 'You request of me more than I am able to offer, Miss Andrews...' He held up his hand to prevent a further torrent of invective. 'I will tell you what I believe to be true, but you will allow me to keep my unproven theories to myself until circumstances validate them or not.'

'Very well,' she replied coolly, her stance remaining stiff and unyielding.

'Did you accompany your father on the Henntawy expedition?'

A puzzled frown touched Miss Andrews' brow. 'No, but I know all about it, and I helped him prepare the exhibits for the British Museum. What has this to do with my father's disappearance?'

'Everything! Despite his immense knowledge of Egyptology, your father was never able to arrive at a comprehensible interpretation of the Henntawy papyrus.'

'Ah, no. It drove him to distraction.'

'He knew there was a missing key?'

Our visitor allowed her stern features to relax into a wry grin. 'He had considered the possibility, yes, along with many others.'

'Did he discuss the papyrus with Sir George Faversham, his partner on the expedition?'

'No. They saw each other as rivals: both were determined to be the first to solve the riddle. Sir George was always claiming that he had succeeded and would send my father taunting telegrams. "Let the man gloat," my father said. "If he really had the answer, he would not tell a soul and would be off to Egypt with the speed of the Devil to get his hands on the Scroll of the Dead."'

'Boasting leads to burglary and murder, eh, Watson?'

'I'm sorry, Holmes. You have lost me.'

'A newspaper report you read out to me only yesterday – when, if you recall, you were trying to rouse my spirits with what I wrongly surmised was a trivial piece of villainy. Sir George Faversham's house was ransacked but nothing of value taken. You recall?'

'Yes, yes I do – and he was murdered.'

'Ah! So the canvas grows broader.' The miscreants were no doubt hoping that Sir George would help them translate the key in order that they could interpret the Henntawy papyrus. When he was unable, or perhaps refused, to do so – they... eliminated him.' He rubbed his hands vigourously. 'You see, Miss Andrews, there are certain unscrupulous individuals desperate to get their hands on Setaph's Scroll of the Dead and they will go to any lengths – including murder – to obtain it. I am sure that the Henntawy papyrus your father was working on, containing the details of the Scroll's whereabouts, was useless without the key – one prepared by Setaph himself. I believe that these people I speak of have obtained the key.'

At this juncture I interrupted. 'If that is the case, why are they not seeking the location of the Scroll of the Dead?'

'Ah, my dear Watson, because like myself, they underestimated the cunning of Setaph. The key also presents puzzles which need solving. Obviously they are not as taxing as the papyrus from the museum, but clever enough to baffle a simple and untutored mind.'

'I think I see what you are implying, Mr Holmes. These villains, of whom you speak, need my father to interpret this key for them.'

'That is how I read the mystery. That is why no ransom is required.'

'If you are correct – what happens to my father when he has done their work for them?'

Holmes paused for a moment, stroking his chin. 'My answer can only be a surmise; but knowing what I do about your father's abductors, I believe they will hold on to him until they have Setaph's Scroll of the

Dead in their grasp. Only then can they be sure your father has provided them with the correct information.'

Miss Andrews slumped back in the chair. I threw a concerned glance at Holmes.

'By which time,' he continued in a lighter tone, 'Doctor Watson and I will have caught up with them.'

'Do you really think so?' Miss Andrews' desperate question exactly mirrored the one I had framed in my own mind.

'I think so,' said Holmes. Our visitor missed the sense of ambiguity in his reply and smiled.

'Please return my father to me safely, Mr Holmes.' For a brief moment the mask of the confident modern woman slipped, revealing the frightened and vulnerable young girl beneath.

'We shall do all in our power to bring about that happy event,' I said cheerily.

'I echo those sentiments,' said Holmes without a flicker of warmth in his voice.

After Miss Andrews had gone, carrying with her Holmes' assurance that he would contact her once there was any news of her father, I rounded on my friend, releasing some of my pent-up anger. 'It is one thing to keep details from a client, Holmes, but quite another to keep me in the dark.'

'My dear fellow, calm down. Please don't blame me if events, and therefore my mental processes, move faster than I had anticipated.'

'How can I be of any use if you do not confide in me?'

'But you know all, Watson. What is there to confide?'

'You talked of villains – in the plural. Who are they? With Melmoth dead...'

'Ah, well, confide I will, but explain the obvious I will not. If I do, however will you learn?'

'Holmes...' I began.

'For goodness' sake, do not look so crestfallen. I know you are a man of action, and tonight there will be some action in which I shall require your assistance.'

'What action?'

'We are going to burgle Melmoth's house,' Sherlock Holmes announced grandly, before lighting his pipe and settling back in his chair.

Six

NIGHT WORK

It was not the first time that Sherlock Holmes had involved me in breaking the law. However, the adventure my friend offered on this occasion seemed to me to be outrageous.

'Burgle Melmoth's house,' I repeated with some scorn. 'You cannot expect me to take your suggestion seriously.'

'I do not jest about such matters, my friend. Forget your sensibilities for a moment and consider what an unmitigated scoundrel this Melmoth is – and I choose my verb carefully.'

'You believe the man is still alive?'

Holmes did not answer me directly, but pointed the stem of his pipe in my direction and said, 'With or without your help, I intend to enter his house tonight and find out, for certain, who lies in his coffin.'

I shuddered. 'Great heavens, Holmes, not only is the whole affair dangerous and against the law, it is also positively ghoulish.'

Holmes grinned. 'What better reasons are there for doing it?'

* * *

The lugubrious chimes of Big Ben striking midnight vibrated in the distance as Holmes and I left the warmth of our sitting-room and emerged into the coolness of the night. Despite my reservations concerning this venture, Holmes knew that I could not refuse his entreaty for me to join him. Much to my dismay the contents of my medical bag had been removed and replaced with a jemmy, a dark lantern, a chisel, and my service revolver.

Sometime in the late afternoon my friend had left Baker Street dressed as respectable, grey-haired, short-sighted clergyman to conduct a full reconnaissance of Melmoth's premises. 'No one is suspicious of a bumbling cleric even though he peers at houses in an unusual fashion,' grinned Holmes on his return, as he released himself from his disguise.

The thoroughfares of the great city were all but deserted. We passed a few late night revellers, and the occasional hansom clip-clopped its way past us, no doubt on its way back to the depot, but otherwise we owned the darkened streets. We walked briskly in silence, my mind astir with worries and apprehensions, while Holmes' face remained taut and exultant with anticipation.

Within fifteen minutes we were close to our destination. We paused in the shadows opposite the house we had visited together that morning, now presenting a blank, dark face to us. None of the windows were lighted and there were no signs of occupancy.

'There is a small garden at the rear of the house. By scaling the wall surrounding it, we shall then be able enter the premises by means of one of the downstairs windows.' Holmes spoke quickly and in a matter of fact tone, as though he were choosing items from a menu.

I began to feel very uneasy. 'What if we are caught?' I asked in a harsh whisper.

'That eventuality is not within my purview,' came the curt reply.

We crossed the road and moved to the side of the house. A solitary gas lamp emitting a meagre glow stood sentry at the top of the narrow lane which ran behind Melmoth's villa. Holmes led me down the lane beyond the feeble gleam of the lamp, and then we stopped by an old, rustic brick wall some ten feet high. 'Now I'll give you a hand up, and when you have secured a hold on the top of the wall I'll pass your bag up to you.'

I sighed heavily. 'Are you sure this is really necessary?'

'Of course it is. Now let's be about our business.'

Having neither the litheness nor the athletic ability of my youth, it took me some time to establish firm foot and hand holds to enable me to clamber to the top of the wall, retrieve my medical bag from Holmes' outstretched hand, and then reach the comparative safety of *terra firma* on the other side. Holmes had no such difficulty. He scaled the wall with ease, and I was still catching my breath from my exertions when he jumped nimbly to the ground and joined me. Advancing towards the house, he lit the bull's-eye lantern. Its narrow beam traced the outline of the building. There was one door to the left, probably leading to the kitchen or the cellars, a centrally-placed short flight of steps up to the main back door, and a veranda which led to a large bow window to the right of it.

Holmes led the way up the steps and nodded in the direction of the bay window. 'That will be our point of entry,' he whispered, thrusting the lantern into my hands. 'A steady beam now, while I get to work with the chisel.'

With the skill of a practised burglar, my companion slipped the chisel into the lower edge of the sash window. I saw him stoop and strain with quick deliberate motions until with a splintering crack it jerked open.

Without delay we climbed through into the house and stood like statues in the gloom, our senses alert to catch the slightest sound or movement. There was nothing: the silence of the house hissed in my ear.

After some moments, Holmes leaned close to me and spoke softly. 'No doubt the coffin will be laid out in one of the rooms on the ground floor – probably the morning-room. Come.' Grasping my sleeve, he tugged me gently, guiding me through the darkness towards the door. He had a remarkable facility, carefully cultivated, for seeing in the dark, and with the aid of the beam from his lantern he was able with cat-like proficiency to manoeuvre our way with ease. Within seconds we were standing in the hallway. A pale luminescence filtered through the fanlight above the front door and threw streaky, shifting shadows down the walls. Again we halted and listened. The stillness was broken gently by the muted ticking of a grandfather clock which stood at the far end of the hall. Holmes swung the beam of the dark lantern, exploring the surroundings. On the hall table, below a garishly ornate mirror, stood a huge bowl of white orchids, pale and ghostly in the gloom: a floral tribute to the dead, no doubt.

There were several doors leading off from the hallway and we tried two, peering over the thresholds as the pale finger of illumination exposed the interiors. They were the music-room and the sitting-room. Our third attempt brought us to the chamber for which we had been searching. To call it a morning-room would be a cruel misnomer. Even in the dim light afforded us by the lantern, I could see that the room was normally a gloomy one. The drapes were black velvet edged with gold and the wallpaper was strange and dismal. It featured a weird set of patterns, engravings almost, picturing a series of grinning, repulsive faces, demonic and gargoyle-like. The sickly-sweet smell of incense, evocative of the east, permeated the air with a thick, cloying aroma that was almost suffocating in its intensity. The luxuriant carpet and furniture appeared to be in various shades of grey, black, or dark brown and, hanging over the mantelpiece, was a portrait of the owner of the house. The oil painting was in the high Gothic style, showing Sebastian Melmoth standing in the moonlight with a ruined castle battlement in the background. His pale face glared out at us with spectral animosity as though the painting were alive and he was aware that we were intruding upon his private quarters. The eyes glittered, animated by hate as the beam of light passed over the face. It was an unnerving apparition.

However, all these observations took but a matter of seconds, for the real interest of this apartment was the dark oak casket resting on trestles in the centre of the room.

Holmes swung the beam of the lantern on to the lid, illuminating a small silver plate, engraved with the legend: *Sebastian Melmoth Hic reviviscere 1866–1896.*

My friend gave a snort of disgust. 'Come Watson, help me with the lid.'

'But surely, Holmes...'

'This is the *raison d'être* of our visit. A closed coffin is no proof. It could easily be empty.'

It was not empty. Despite all the bloodshed and the grisly injuries I had witnessed during my time in Afghanistan, I could not prevent my gorge from rising at the sight we witnessed as the lid was removed from the coffin. Perhaps, I pondered later, it was the incongruity of it that shocked my system. Despite being informed that Melmoth had been killed in a shooting accident, I was unprepared for the horrific extent of his wound. The mutilated corpse lay in the coffin with his wounds clearly on view. The upper half of his chest had been blown away and he had no face to speak of – just a mask of gory, dark red tissue which glistened in the light. Even the head had been shaved of its blond locks, further enhancing its ghoulish appearance.

Holmes was far from taken aback by the sight of the apparition that lay before us. In fact he gave a murmur of satisfaction. 'A hunting accident, eh? Well it would have taken at least two cartridges to create this effect. It has been very nicely done, Watson. Very nicely done indeed.' So saying he leaned over the corpse and examined the hands closely; then, shining the lamp on to what had once been a face, he scrutinised the teeth protruding from the ghastly mask of raw flesh.

'Well, I am quite convinced that whoever this fellow is, he is certainly not Sebastian Melmoth.'

'How can you be so certain?'

'The evidence here merely proves what I already suspected. Look at the hands...' He lifted one up and shone the lamp on to it. 'Observe the callouses, the dirt-ingrained fingernails. These are not the hands of an aesthete and dandy; they are the hands of a labourer.' Dropping the arm, he leaned further over the corpse and pulled back the shreds of flesh around the mouth. 'Similarly the teeth have not had the benefit of the expensive dental care that the rich can afford. Those brown and black stumps speak of an unhealthy diet and neglect. No, my friend, this poor devil is merely a substitute, a decoy, if you like, to disguise the fact that Sebastian Melmoth is still very much alive.'

'But what is the purpose behind this deception?'

'I may flatter myself, but I believe it has been done mainly for my benefit, to put me off the scent. If the major suspect is dead, then the detective has to look elsewhere for another...'

'Meanwhile, he carries on with his nefarious plans with impunity.'

'Exactly.'

'But who then is this wretch in the coffin?'

I was destined not to receive the answer to my query for, as Holmes was about to reply, there came a noise from the upper part of the house. It was the sound of voices. My heart sank. Someone had heard us.

Immediately Holmes extinguished the lantern. 'Quickly,' he whispered harshly, 'help me close the coffin.'

Like blind men we wrestled with the coffin lid, slotting it back in place in the cloistered darkness. As we completed our macabre task, I heard footsteps coming down the stairs. I virtually froze to the spot, but Holmes dragged me over to the window and pulled me behind the heavy black drapes. As he did so the room was bathed in electric light.

Someone entered. From the sound of the heavy tread and the lengthy strides I took it to be a man. I heard him move to the coffin, cocking a pistol as he did so. His measured tread grew nearer and I could sense him coming closer to our hiding place. Holmes held his finger to his lip.

And then the drapes stirred as though a hand had been placed on them – a hand which at any second would expose us. The inside of my mouth suddenly became very dry and my heart began to race.

Just as I was fearing the worst, there came the muffled cry of a woman from one of the other rooms.

'What is it, Julia?' cried the fellow, less than two feet away from us.

'Someone has broken in, Brandon: the window in the dining-room has been forced open.'

Holmes mouthed the word 'Butler' to me.

'I'm coming,' said the man, the curtains shuddering as he released his grasp. We heard him leave.

'Now is the time for us to make *our* exit,' muttered Holmes and, wielding the chisel with dexterous aplomb, he forced up the window behind us. With as much speed as we could muster, we climbed over the window-sill and slipped out once again into the cold night air. Noiselessly, Holmes drew the window down, and within seconds we were on the pavement walking steadily in the direction of Baker Street with all the casual nonchalance of two late night revellers making their way home.

'Well,' remarked Holmes, as we turned the corner into Baker Street, 'we must away to our beds as quickly as possible. We shall have to be up betimes: a long train journey lies ahead of us tomorrow.'

I groaned. 'Where to?'

'Norfolk,' came the reply.

Seven

A COUNTRY INTERLUDE

Dawn was breaking, chill and grey, as the train pulled out of Liverpool Street Station early that same morning. I had been too tired and drained of energy to question both the reason and the need for this sojourn before going to bed in an attempt to snatch a few hours' rest. However, I believed that I had some notion of Holmes' plans, and I thought that a night's refreshing sleep would sharpen the brain and bring the whole picture into focus. I was wrong. For a start I managed but four hours' sleep. Holmes was shaking my shoulder and rousing me at five. 'Come along, Watson, we have a train to catch. Never let it be said that the old hounds were slow to lead the chase.'

'Old hounds,' I murmured drowsily, still hugging my pillow. 'Haven't you heard the saying about letting sleeping dogs lie?'

Holmes replied with a sound that fell somewhere between a laugh and a snort. 'We leave in half an hour,' he cried, slamming the door behind him.

Once the train had left the confines of London, a pale, watery sun struggled to make an appearance in the slate-coloured sky and I managed finally to shrug off the lethargy of sleep. 'I presume,' I said, addressing my friend, who was sitting huddled in the corner of our First Class compartment, staring out of the window and smoking a cigarette, 'that our visit to Norwich is connected with the shooting accident on Lord Felshaw's estate.'

'Quite right, Watson. The young man whom we saw yesterday at Melmoth's place was so over-confident that he rather foolishly gave us too much information for his own good. Tobias Felshaw, another of the decadent Melmoth crowd.'

'And you suspect him of involvement in this affair?'

'Right up to his corrupt, aristocratic neck.'

'Melmoth's accomplice.'

'Yes. The pair of them now have three murders on their heads.'

'Three?'

'Daventry, the night watchman; Sir George Faversham; and the poor devil who now lies in Melmoth's coffin.'

'You really think that they murdered Sir George because he could not or would not help them?'

'Quite right, Watson. No doubt they approached him first with Setaph's key, asking him for help in deciphering it with the promise of... well, any treasures found along with the Scroll of the Dead.' Holmes gave a dry chuckle. 'It was somewhat naive of them to make the approach directly; when Sir George failed to oblige them, for whatever reason, they had no option but to kill him.'

'Because he knew their secret.'

'Exactly.'

I shuddered at the thought of such a cold-blooded murder and then brought to mind the pale, cruel face of Melmoth with that absurd, maniacal glitter in his eyes. 'There is something inhuman about that kind of calculated butchery,' I said.

'These are evil men, Watson. They delight in their sin for its own sake.'

'You think we will find them at Holden Hall?'

Holmes narrowed his eyes and blew out a thin wisp of smoke. 'I cannot say for certain how events will fall out; but I am convinced that we shall find something to our advantage.'

Holden Hall was some twenty miles out of the old cathedral city of Norwich, so we hired a pony and trap at the station and drove ourselves. After a pleasant spell along some country roads, we entered the village of Holden Parva and I espied the village inn, The Blacksmith's Arms. 'My stomach tells me it's lunch time, Holmes,' I said, indicating the hostelry. 'I've had nothing to eat since breakfast at six this morning, and that was only a tepid cup of coffee and a piece of toast.'

To my surprise, Holmes acquiesced to my request without objection. Tying our horse to a large iron ring fixed into the wall outside the inn, we entered. It was a rough and ready place with stone floors and simple wooden benches and stools, but all looked clean and tidy and the landlord, a short, dark-haired fellow, bade us a cheery welcome. We secured ourselves some bread, cheese and pickle, and a tankard of ale and sat at one of the benches to consume our fare. There were several other customers, men in rustic dress – moleskin trousers, gaiters, leather jerkins, and broad belts. A little knot of them leaned on the bar, deep in conversation with the landlord.

Holmes remained silent throughout our meal, but he was observing all about him with careful scrutiny. When we had devoured the last of the cheese, the landlord came over to collect our plates.

'That was just what the doctor ordered,' said Holmes cheerily, giving me a sly grin. 'Tell me, landlord, I couldn't help hearing you talking about the dreadful shooting accident that occurred up at the Hall a few days ago.'

The rosy features of the innkeeper lost some of their colour. 'You've heard about it then, have you sir? My, ain't it surprisin' how news travels?'

'I had business up at the Hall with Lord Felshaw's son and I was told he was away attending a funeral. That is how I came to know of the shooting.'

'Aye, it's a wicked affair,' cried one of the men at the bar, who boasted a full thatch of yellow hair with a matching beard that was in danger of engulfing his whole face. 'It may be wrong of me to say so, but those two, young master Tobias and his peculiar friend, have been asking for some disaster to fall upon their heads for some time.'

'I take it that the "young master" is not liked?'

This remark provoked a chorus of guffaws.

'You can say that again, sir,' grinned the landlord. 'Apart from anythin' else, he ain't natural.' He winked grotesquely at Holmes. 'If you get my meanin'. Not what you'd call... a man.'

Holmes responded with an expression of shrewd comprehension.

'Always having strange parties and the like up at the Hall,' chipped in another fellow at the bar, while the others nodded, all apparently warming to a favourite topic of conversation.

'He was cruel, too,' added the fellow with the yellow beard. 'On one occasion he thrashed a groom for not saddling his horse properly. He was hurt so bad the poor fellow nearly died. His lordship's father had the whole thing hushed up and the chap was paid handsomely not to bring charges.'

'This Tobias appears to be a very unpleasant customer,' observed Holmes darkly. 'I begin to think that I was fortunate that he was away when I called. He sounds somewhat unstable.'

'When you've money,' announced a whippet-faced fellow with slurred speech, the one in the group who seemed to have consumed more beer than the rest, 'when you've money, you can get away with murder.'

There was a sudden silence and Holmes' eyes twinkled merrily. 'You're not saying there was something amiss about the shooting accident, are you?' he asked casually, smiling at the men.

They glanced at each other, apparently tongue-tied.

'Well, let's put it like this, mister,' whippet-face announced suddenly, 'we've only got his lordship's words as to what went on. He has the Devil's own temper and I wouldn't put it past him to have shot his friend over some argument or other.'

'Shut up, now, Nathan,' said the bearded drinker quietly, nudging his companion in the ribs.

But Holmes was not going to let it stop there. The momentum was going nicely, and I could tell from his expression that he was aware there was more to know and that he wanted to know it. 'But surely,' he said in warm tones, as though he were an old friend of theirs, 'there is the testimony of the estate worker who was with them when the accident happened.'

Whippet-face laughed. 'Good point, sir. Good point. Only young Alfred's done a bunk.'

'You mean he's disappeared?'

'We reckon it's like Thompson the groom all over again. He's been paid to go away and be quiet,' said the landlord softly as he moved back to the bar.

'He's not been seen around the estate since the accident,' said whippet-face.

'What about at home?' I asked.

'He lives on his own, has a little cottage on the estate, down by the lake.'

'Look, gentlemen, isn't it time we changed the conversation, eh?' said the landlord nervously. 'Too much talk about the goings on up at the Hall and it's likely to bring a curse on the Inn.'

'The only curse I've got is the missus,' moaned whippet-face miserably; and then suddenly his face cracked into a wide beam as an infectious high-pitched whinny of merriment escaped his lips, causing his companions to laugh along with him. The tension was dispelled and they turned away from us and began to indulge in merry banter about whose turn it was to buy the next round of drinks.

Holmes leaned over and whispered in my ear. 'You are invaluable on a case, Watson. Your suggestion to take lunch here was a master stroke.'

We left The Blacksmith's Arms to the accompaniment of a series of nods and mumbled farewells from our lunch-time companions.

'What those poor devils don't know is that young Alfred hasn't done a bunk with some loot,' remarked Holmes once we had climbed aboard our trap. 'He's the corpse at Melmoth's funeral today.'

I felt a sudden chill at the thought of the heartless nerve required to contemplate and plan such an atrocious act, let alone carry it out.

'I had deduced these facts while still in London,' admitted my friend, 'and although it is satisfying to have things confirmed, there is a greater purpose to our sojourn.'

'Which is?'

'To test out a little theory of mine.'

I was well aware that it was useless to enquire what this theory was. I knew my friend of old and how he loved to surprise me in his theatrical manner by revealing at the eleventh hour some remarkable development in the investigation. He would explain it all at the time it suited him and not before, despite any pleas from me. If I had learned anything from my years with Sherlock Holmes, it was patience.

We continued our journey to Holden Hall, leaving all signs of habitation behind. We became enveloped in a green world of rustling, budding greenery, birdsong and animal calls – a natural world far removed from the greed and cruelty of mankind. I had slipped into a reverie about man's inhumanity to man when Holmes nudged my elbow and pointed. Through the trees, I observed in the distance a great house, with a large stretch of water beyond.

'There lies our destination.'

'The lake?'

My companion smiled. 'Not quite. Alfred's cottage. Remember our loquacious friend back at the inn informed us that his cottage was down by the lake. Now, in order to make our visit less public, we'll slip over the wall yonder and follow the line of trees, using it as a screen, until we reach the water.'

'What if we're spotted – apprehended? There must be a game-keeper on patrol.'

'I will think of something, never fear.'

'We may not be given the opportunity to explain ourselves.'

'You always look on the black side, Watson. You have your revolver with you, haven't you? Good. Now do come on.'

Leaving the horse and trap off the road behind a thicket, we clambered over the low wall and entered the grounds of Holden Hall.

By now it was two in the afternoon and the early promise of a fine spring day was dwindling. Amorphous grey clouds were forming in the sky, gradually but relentlessly blocking out any trace of the pale eggshell blue. The breeze had also stiffened, rattling the branches above our heads, shaking the new green shoots wildly.

There was no given path and so we aimed ourselves in the direction of the lake and set off. After travelling some three hundred yards through the wood, the thick, green undergrowth pressing in on us from both sides, Holmes stopped and pulled an eyeglass from his coat. Then he passed it to me, indicating where I should look. I moved the eyeglass slowly across the terrain beyond the trees, scanning the grey choppy waters of the lake, then shifted my gaze to the greensward on shore and up towards the bank of trees on the horizon. It was then that I observed it: a little cottage perched on the edge of the wood above the lake. It was a small, ramshackle building of honey-coloured stone. The garden appeared to be overgrown and the windows were bleared with dirt. 'Alfred's cottage,' I whispered.

'It must be. Observe how the wood curves around behind it. We can make our way to the rear of the building by continuing to use the trees as a screen,' he said, pocketing his telescope. 'Come along, Watson, the game's afoot.' And with this utterance, he was off at great speed through the undergrowth.

As we moved through the trees in line with the sweep of the lake, we heard a gunshot echo in the woods behind us. We dropped to the ground and listened. Moments later there was another sharp crack of gunfire.

'There *is* a gamekeeper about,' I whispered harshly.

'And going about his appointed task, by the sound of it,' remarked Holmes with a tight smile. 'Those shots were a fair distance away. Provided we keep our senses alert, we should have no difficulty escaping his notice.'

We waited in silence for some little time but heard no further noise of gunfire, and so we recommenced our trek through the undergrowth. As we moved, I strained my ears to pick up any unusual sound, anything to signal that danger was near, but apart from the wind through the trees and the occasional animal noise, I heard nothing of significance.

Within ten minutes we had reached the section of the wood directly behind the cottage. The building appeared still and empty. There was no smoke spiralling from its drunken chimney pot and no sight nor sound to suggest that it was occupied.

'I hope we are doing the right thing, Holmes. What if it belongs to some other estate worker?'

Holmes ignored my remark and motioned me to follow him out of the wood, down towards the cottage. With some misgivings, I followed.

There was a low wall and some outbuildings at the rear of the property, and a pen which at one time had obviously contained chickens. Holmes instructed me to stay by the wall while he, crouching low, crept up to the window and peered over the sill. He turned to me and shook his head. 'You stay there and keep out of sight,' he hissed, 'and I will take a look around the front.'

Before I had the opportunity to reply, my companion had disappeared down the side of the house. With a resigned shrug of the shoulders, I knelt down in the damp grass by the wall and waited. Time ticked by with no signs of movement in the house. A fine drizzle now began to fall and I tensed at every small noise: the creaking and rustle of the trees behind me, the unrecognisable cry of some woodland creature, and the wail of the wind as it swept around the corners of the cottage. The old cottage stared back at me blankly, the dirty windows and the begrimed door revealing none of its secrets.

After a time, impatience overcame all other considerations. I rose to my feet, intent on following Holmes around to the front of the cottage, when suddenly the rear door began to move. I dropped to my knees again and watched. At first the handle trembled indignantly and then started to turn with a rusty creak. I held my breath as the door juddered away from the warped frame and began to open, reluctantly, an inch at a time. Automatically, my hand reached into my coat pocket for my revolver as a dark figure, its face in shadow, was revealed in the doorway.

'Sorry to have kept you waiting,' came a voice, obviously addressing me. 'Do come in.'

Eight

THE SECRET OF THE COTTAGE

The dark figure emerged from the doorway into the daylight. It was Sherlock Holmes.

'Come out, Watson,' he said. 'There is no further need to remain in hiding.'

My friend ushered me into the cottage, pushing the door back into its weather-warped frame so that it closed behind us. He must have read the concern in my face, for he patted me on the back reassuringly. 'Don't look so worried, Watson. There is no one here other than us.'

'A wasted journey, then.'

'On the contrary,' beamed Holmes, 'this place is a real treasure house. Come, let me show you.'

Taking my arm, he led me into a small kitchen. In the centre stood a rough wooden table on which lay a mouldy chunk of bread, three dirty tin plates, and some crockery. Over the grate hung a large greasy pot which contained the congealed dregs of some foul concoction.

'Rather a lot of dirty dishes for one estate worker, don't you think?' Holmes said, pointedly.

'A lazy estate worker. It is obvious that he has not washed up for some time.'

'Not quite. Scrutiny of these plates reveals that they contain the remains of the same meal.'

'What are you suggesting?'

'On examining the debris here,' he said, picking up what looked like the bones of a rabbit from one of the plates, 'it seems clear that two people have partaken of this rabbit stew. Two plates, two mugs, and two sets of cutlery.' He dropped the bone and it clattered noisily onto the plate.

'Two people. But who?'

'Come, Watson. Use your brain. Who has need to hide out here?'

'I suppose you mean Melmoth. Alfred gets the coffin, and Melmoth inherits the cottage where he can lie low for a while.'

Holmes nodded. 'And...?'

'It can't be Tobias Felshaw. He was in London yesterday and he will be at the funeral today.'

'Indeed. So who is the other character in this puzzle who remains missing?'

I thought for a moment, and then the answer came to me in a blinding flash. 'You can't mean Miss Andrews' father, Sir Alistair?' I cried.

'Bull's eye,' he cried, rubbing his hands together with enthusiasm. 'Good man. Yes, of course. An ideal place to hold him as a prisoner until they forced him to decipher Setaph's key and then the stolen papyrus. There are two beds upstairs: both have been slept in, but one still has rope tied to its head, obviously where Sir Alistair was secured during the night. And then there is this...'

Again he took my arm and pulled me into the tiny front parlour of the cottage. The only furniture in the room was an ancient sofa and a threadbare armchair pulled up to the tiny fireplace. Holmes leaned over the side of this chair and scooped up a handful of crumpled papers which had been lying on the floor by its side.

'Look at these,' he said, grinning and thrusting them in my hand.

I took them over to the curtainless window where the grey light filtering through the smears afforded me enough illumination to examine the papers. They did not really make sense to me, but I could see that they contained a variety of Egyptian hieroglyphics. As I gazed at them in complete puzzlement, the full import of Holmes' implications came forcefully to me.

'They are not idle scribblings, but a systematic working out of images – hieroglyphics. The sheets provide incontrovertible proof that Sir Alistair Andrews has been here and that he has been working on Setaph's key,' he announced with glee. 'Each one of them possesses his little idiosyncratic signature of Thoth in the corner.'

I observed the crude sketch of the ibis-headed god, identical to the one Miss Andrews had shown us on her father's letter.

Suddenly Holmes' mood changed and he smacked his hand down on the chair. 'I've been slow, Watson. Painfully slow. If we had arrived yesterday, judging by the state of that stew, we would have caught our birds in their new nest. But now they have flown.'

'What about Sir Alistair? You don't think they have killed him, do you?'

My friend shook his head. 'They cannot afford to be rid of him until the Scroll of the Dead is in their hands. He could quite easily have tricked them with his translation. They are too clever, too cautious, to risk that. Oh no, they will keep him close to them until their diabolical quest is at an end. That is our one consolation. Hallo, what have we here?'

Holmes leaned over the armchair and from down the side of the ancient cushion he pulled out a small slip of paper. He joined me by the window to examine it. At first glance, the paper appeared to be another sheet of Sir Alistair's notes, but on closer examination, I could see that the designs were obviously not Egyptian.

'What have we here?' repeated Holmes slowly, more to himself than to me. He pondered some minutes, turning the paper in different directions until he let out a whoop of joy.

'Of course! of course!' he cried. 'The gods have indeed been helpful to us – or at least Sir Alistair has!'

'What do you mean?'

'Look at it, Watson. Cunning little designs.' I looked over my friend's shoulder at the paper. There were several crude, simplistic sketches on it.

'What do you make of it, Watson?'

'Not much – aimless scribbles,' I replied.

'Scribbles I grant you. But they hold a message. Tell me what you see.'

'Well, there appears to be a little house. One of the windows has been blacked out; then there is a set of stairs and some kind of jug and what looks like a coffin.'

'Not an ordinary coffin...'

'No, no. You're right. It is an Egyptian coffin: a sarcophagus.'

Holmes held out his hand, waiting for more. I had no more to give.

'I see – or rather I don't see,' I said. 'Obviously you believe that these drawings have some significance.'

'I believe they do – and we can soon find out.'

'How?'

Holmes chuckled. 'Follow me. If I have this right, the cryptic little note was left by Melmoth's hostage in case anyone should discover this bolthole.'

By now Holmes was bounding up the stairs with myself close on his heels. On the narrow landing he stopped and consulted the drawing again. 'Two bedrooms only upstairs. See, the window at the top left in the sketch is the one blacked out, so it must be this bedroom.' He darted off into the room on the left and rushed to the window with a cry of delight. 'Our jug,' he exclaimed, and from the window sill he snatched a grubby willow pattern water jug which resembled the child-like sketch on the paper. He turned it upside down in expectation that something would fall out. Nothing did. A flicker of consternation crossed his brow and hesitantly he slipped his hand inside the jug. 'Ah!' he cried, in triumph, 'there is something in here, pressed tightly against the inner wall.'

Still with his hand inside the jug, he moved to the fireplace and smashed the ornament down on the blackleaded mantelpiece. There was an explosion of china, with little blue shards flying off in all directions. With another cry of satisfaction, he pulled out two sheets of paper from the debris and examined them carefully. 'Treasure trove indeed, Watson.'

'What are they?'

'Rough copies. But very precious rough copies. I believe one is a copy of the key to the Henntawy papyrus and the other is a copy of the papyrus itself.'

He handed them to me, and although I could determine that they represented a series of Egyptian designs, with crude representations of figures, animals, and symbols, the sense was impenetrable.

'Don't you see?' cried Holmes, his voice high with excitement. 'Sir Alistair has left this behind in order to help in tracking him down... and his kidnappers. He has left behind as much information as his captors possess.'

'But how could he have known that anyone would come looking for him here?'

Holmes smiled to himself the way he always did when his understanding of the situation was greater than mine. 'Let's say it was the act of a drowning man grasping at straws. However, he would have known that his strong-willed daughter would not have simply stayed at home doing nothing, while he was being held prisoner somewhere. He knew she would set some hounds on his trail.' He waved the two sheets of paper in the air. 'And just in case...'

'But why leave the key and not the solution?'

Holmes shrugged. 'Perhaps because he has not revealed all the details to Melmoth and young Felshaw. For as long as he is useful to them, his life is safe. It would be foolish to leave the full solution where it was possible they might stumble over it. And, of course, he may not have solved the puzzles of either the key or the stolen papyrus.'

'That makes sense,' I agreed, 'but it does not help us much, as we still have to solve the puzzles also.'

Surprisingly, Holmes grinned broadly. 'To the author of a trifling monograph upon the subject of secret writings in which I analysed one hundred and sixty separate ciphers, this ancient riddle-me-ree should not prove too challenging.' My look of disbelief, prompted by this arrogant statement, caused Holmes to burst out in one of his rare fits of laughter. 'Have a little faith,' he cried at last, stifling his guffaws.

'I think we shall need a little more than faith,' said I.

Some time later, after Holmes had searched the cottage for further clues to ensure that he had not overlooked anything else of significance, we began our return to the waiting pony and trap. We were in the thickest part of the wood, where we had to push ourselves with some effort through the foliage, when, without warning, Holmes pushed me to the ground into a patch of tall, wet grass. He landed beside me and, before I had chance to react, he had clamped his fingers across my mouth to stifle any utterance I might make. 'Gamekeeper,' he whispered in my ear, and released his grip.

I followed the line of his gaze and saw a thickset fellow in country tweeds some fifty yards away from us. He was carrying a twin-barrelled shot gun.

'I don't think he has seen us, but he certainly seems to be looking for something or someone. We had best stay put unless he comes too close, and then we shall have to make a run for it,' said Holmes.

Despite our stealth, in all probability we had been spotted outside Alfred's cottage, and the gamekeeper was now trying to pick up our trail. He had been standing motionless like an animal for a while, sensing the air; then he turned in our direction and began walking towards us. As he drew nearer I could see that he was a red-faced brute of a man with two small, mean eyes set under a shaggy blond brow. He shifted his gun to his shoulder and aimed it at a nearby tree, and then swung it round in a semi-circle as though he was looking for a target. He moved nearer, his heavy boots crunching the covering of dry bracken and twigs on the woodland floor as he did so. My heart began to race. I felt sure that at any time he would discover us and blast us both to kingdom come. He certainly did not look the sort of fellow who would bother to question our presence on the estate: in his eyes we were trespassers, and therefore fair game. Instinctively my hand reached for my gun, although I reminded myself that it would be wholly inappropriate for me to to use it unless we were faced with the direst consequences. Once again Holmes and I had placed ourselves on the wrong side of the law, and therefore we were the miscreants in the matter.

I pushed myself down as flat as I could into the long grass, while still keeping an eye on the gamekeeper's progress. Suddenly the air was rent with a strange animal noise – a high-pitched rasping cry. It came from far to our left, cutting sharply through the sound of the rustling leaves. This stopped our gamekeeper in his tracks and he froze like some rustic statue. He waited a few moments and then the cry came again. This time he turned and hared off in the direction of the sound.

'There are two of them,' said Holmes at length, after our adversary had disappeared from sight. 'That was a calling signal from his partner. Opportune for us. Another minute and I believe we would have made the very unpleasant acquaintance of the man and his gun.'

'The sooner we are away from here the better,' I said, clambering to my feet and brushing myself down.

Holmes grinned. 'Sentiments with which I heartily concur.'

Without further ado, we resumed our trek to the edge of the estate. We were much more cautious and apprehensive than we had been now that we had come into contact with the tangible danger that lay in wait for us in the wood. However, we had not gone more than 400 yards when we heard a voice call out to us, 'Stop, you rascals, or I fire!'

I turned around on the instant and caught a glimpse through the greenery of another figure in tweeds carrying a twin-bore. He was taller and less broad than the first, but his demeanour was as threatening.

'Keep going,' hissed Holmes.

Before I had chance to respond, there was a loud explosion and the small branch above my head cracked and fell to the ground.

'Heavens, he means to kill us,' I gasped, stumbling forward.

'We are vermin to him, no doubt,' observed Holmes in a sharp whisper, 'but that shot was too wide to be a serious threat. He's just out to frighten us. Keep down and keep moving.'

I did as I was bidden.

Another shot rang out and I felt my hat fly from my head.

'That was serious enough for me,' I said, stumbling forward and picking up my hat. Part of the rim was missing and a large, charred scar ran along the band.

We struggled through the dense undergrowth, stumbling over fallen branches and being pulled by wayward brambles, until we emerged into a clearing and were able to increase our speed. In the distance, I could see the road beckoning. Our last lap. Glimpsing a path that appeared to lead to the edge of the estate, we headed down it at full pelt, but I was conscious that our pursuer was still doggedly on our tails. Glancing ahead I saw with horror that our way was blocked by the red-faced keeper, who must have raced ahead of us, using another track. At the sight of us, his florid features curled into a vicious grin.

'Hold it there, gents,' he cried with a sneer, levelling the gun at Holmes. Without thinking, I threw my hat with some force at his face. It caught him on the bridge of the nose and he staggered back in surprise. As he did so, Holmes leapt forward and placed a smart uppercut on his chin. The keeper fell backwards, cracking his head on the trunk of an oak tree. His eyes rolled, his jaw dropped, and he lost consciousness.

Holmes snatched up the rifle and turned to face our pursuer, who, on seeing the weapon, slowed down to a trot. He stopped altogether as Holmes shifted the rifle to his shoulder and took aim. My friend fired above the fellow's head, the shot echoing like a phantom thunderclap in the air, sending a shower of leaves down upon our pursuer's head. He promptly threw himself onto the ground in terror and then, as Holmes raised the rifle once more, he jumped to his feet and fled the way he had come. Holmes fired a final shot once more into the air as the keeper disappeared from our sight.

Red-face groaned loudly as he slowly regained consciousness.

'Come, Watson, let us make ourselves scarce,' cried Holmes cheerily, throwing the gun down. So saying, he hared off towards the perimeter wall. With a thumping heart, I snatched up the remains of my hat and chased after him.

Nine

COMPLICATIONS

Within two hours of our exploits on the Felshaw estate, Holmes and I were ensconsed in a First Class carriage rattling our way back to London. Our adventure in the woods completely forgotten, my companion sat hunched by the window, poring over the documents he had rescued from the estate cottage, while thick columns of grey smoke rolled from the bowl of his pipe. He scribbled designs and words into his notepad constantly, while muttering occasionally to himself, but he made no attempt whatsoever to communicate with me. I settled back into my seat, resigned to a silent journey, and closed my eyes. Sleep soon overtook me.

When I awoke, night had fallen and the compartment was bathed in the amber glow of two gas mantles. Holmes was still sitting by the window, but now he was gazing out into the blackness of the night, his hawk-like features staring back at him from the darkened pane. The documents lay discarded in his lap. I consulted my watch. We were due to arrive in London in the next forty minutes or so.

'Have you made any sense of the key?' I asked Holmes tentatively.

He turned his gaze on me as though he had just realised that I was there in the compartment with him, so deep were his thoughts. 'I believe so. There are several points which still remain shrouded but I hope that, supplied with a suitably ancient map of Egypt and having made certain enquiries, I shall be able to satisfy myself as to their meaning. As with all things appertaining to Setaph, nothing is quite what it seems.'

'You mean you have broken the code already?'

'Do not be so surprised.'

'Well, I am. If prominent Egyptologists have failed over the years to interpret this document, and you have managed to do it in a matter of hours, it is more than surprising. It is remarkable.'

Holmes gave a grunt. 'That is the over-emotive language of the writer, Watson. Indeed, Egyptologists have addressed the problem of Setaph's code – but they have approached the problem from their perspective as Egyptologists, and not as I have done – with the objective, scientific approach of a code-breaker. Codes, whether written by ancient Egyptians or the man in the moon, have to follow certain set patterns, and it is the isolation of these patterns which is of paramount importance – not the culture or the nationality of the man who created the puzzle.'

'So you know where the Scroll of the Dead lies?'

Holmes gave me a sly grin. 'As I have already intimated, I believe I shall do so when I have consulted a map of Ancient Egypt and satisfied myself as to the accuracy of certain data which I possess.' With this retort, Holmes closed his eyes and feigned sleep.

There was another surprise awaiting us on our return to Baker Street. On entering the hallway of 221B, I nearly fell over a large trunk placed there. As I steadied myself, Mrs Hudson, no doubt disturbed by the noise, appeared in the doorway of her room. 'Oh, gentlemen, here you are at last.' Her voice was anxious and her features furrowed with concern.

'What is it, Mrs Hudson?' asked Holmes in the softest of tones, as he cast a practiced eye over the trunk.

'It's that young lady – the one who was here yesterday. Miss Andrews...'

'What about her?'

'She's here now... in your room... insisting on seeing you.'

'This is her trunk, I take it?'

'Indeed it is, Mr Holmes. I believe she has got it into her head that she is to stay here in this house. I don't know what this is all about, Mr Holmes, but we simply do not have the room for another lodger...'

'Miss Andrews lodge here?' I gasped. 'What can she be thinking of, Holmes?'

My friend could barely conceal the smile that was on his lips. 'Please, don't either of you fret yourselves. I am sure this matter can be sorted out quite easily. However, Mrs Hudson, surely you can make up a bed for the young lady just for tonight?' He consulted the hall clock. 'It is not far from midnight, and it would be callous and imprudent to turn her out onto the streets at this hour. Don't you agree, Watson?'

I failed to reply. I was too dumbfounded.

'Good,' chirped Holmes, taking both my silence and that of Mrs Hudson as acquiescence to his suggestion.

Our landlady gave one of her long, weary sighs. 'Very well, Mr Holmes. One night and one night only.'

'Indeed. Now then, Watson, let's discover what this determined young lady has to say for herself.'

With that he bounded up the stairs towards our sitting room.

As it turned out, our visitor, Miss Catriona Andrews, initially had nothing to say for herself, because she was asleep. I entered the room just behind Holmes, and caught a glimpse of the girl, dressed in the same outfit that she had worn the day before, sitting in my chair by the fire, her head lolling forward on her chest. She was a striking young woman with strong features, and while not handsome in the accepted sense, there was something about the mouth and the eyes and her forthright demeanour that was very appealing. It was a puzzle to me that she had no gentleman friend to help share her burdens. It was clear that her dedication to her father was complete.

'A brandy nightcap for our guest, Watson, and one for myself too if you don't mind.' Holmes threw off his outer clothes and turned up the gas while I busied myself preparing the drinks. The noise of our activity brought the girl back to consciousness. She stirred dreamily at first and then, shaking off her fatigue, was on her feet and staring at my friend.

'At last you've returned, Mr Holmes. What news? Oh, please tell me, what news?'

'Calm yourself, Miss Andrews. Take the brandy from Watson. It will steady your nerves.'

The soft brown eyes turned in my direction, and with a slightly trembling hand she took the tumbler from me. 'Thank you,' she said softly.

'That's better,' murmured Holmes as he sat opposite her. 'Now, before I tell you my news, would you be kind enough to explain your presence here, and why you have decided to give my landlady a fright by bringing your luggage along with you?'

The girl took a sip of her nightcap before replying. On doing so, she looked at my friend with a steady gaze. Her features, having shaken off the softness of sleep, were once more set with a flinty determination. 'I have given a great deal of thought to what you told me on my visit here yesterday. In my mind I ran over the events that led up to my father's disappearance, and I am now completely convinced that you are correct in your supposition: he has been kidnapped because of his special knowledge regarding the Scroll. Therefore the obvious course of action is for us to travel to Egypt to pick up the trail there. That is why I am here, packed and ready to go.'

Holmes' placid expression remained unmoved and he said nothing, but I could not stop myself from interrupting at this point. 'Surely you do not think we would allow you to accompany us on any such journey, Miss Andrews,' I cried. 'There are dangers...' I got no further in my protestations, for the young woman rounded on me, fierce indignation radiating from her eyes.

'Allow!' she retorted harshly. 'Allow! We are not living in the Middle Ages now, Doctor Watson. It is not given to you, or any man, to say what I may or may not do. I am an independent citizen of a democratic country and I can and will do all I wish that is within the boundary of the law, Christian morals, and good manners. Perhaps I ought to consider whether I should "allow" *you* to accompany *me* to Egypt. Remember, I have a great knowledge of the country, its customs, and terrain. I thought that you would have enough good sense to realise what an invaluable companion I could be in this venture.'

'I only meant...' said I, taken aback at the vehemence of Miss Andrews' tirade.

'Like so many men, Doctor Watson, you speak before you consider.'

Holmes afforded himself a light chuckle. 'Call off your dogs, Miss Andrews. I think we take your point. Certainly, one cannot question your tenacity and determination but, pray tell me, why are you so convinced that our search leads us to Egypt?'

'Where else? Setaph's tomb lies there. The men who have kidnapped my father are after the Scroll of the Dead, are they not?'

Holmes nodded.

'Then sooner or later they will go to Egypt. You said that you believed that these despicable creatures would hold on to father until they had Setaph's magical Scroll in their hands.' She paused a moment, the fire in her eyes flickering low. 'Do you still hold that belief?'

'I do.'

'Then there is no point in searching for a needle in a haystack in

England when you know that the Nile basin is the final destination.'

'Miss Andrews, what you say is admirably reasoned. Although I may not have secured the needle in that haystack to which you refer, I have gained more information which will help us to narrow down our field of investigation.'

He face brightened. 'Then please tell me all. If you have information regarding my father's whereabouts, then for pity's sake let me know it.'

Holmes appeared touched by her emotional plea, and he rendered her a concise account, tactfully edited, of our pastoral sojourn to Norfolk. Her cheeks flushed with excitement and she sat forward in her chair like an eager child when her father was mentioned. She was a woman of many dramatic, shifting moods and humours and, chameleon-like, she had a predilection to slip in and out of them as her emotions dictated.

'At least we know that he is still alive,' she sighed wearily, slumping back in her chair, when Holmes had finished.

'Yes... we do.'

'And it proves that you were right in your guesswork about Setaph's Scroll.'

'I know I am only a mere man, Miss Andrews, but as a consulting detective whose methodology is deductive reasoning, I can assure you that I never guess.'

'I apologise. Your plans are now for Egypt?'

There was a long pause as Holmes stared past the girl at the flickering flames of the fire, his brow contracted as though he were caught in a trance. And then, suddenly, he broke from his reverie and addressed the girl briskly. 'Indeed, as you so rightly surmised: Egypt is our destination. Tomorrow we make our arrangements. The sooner we set foot on the desert sand, the sooner this case will be brought to a conclusion and we shall be able to return your father to you.'

'Mr Holmes, I must go with you. I... I insist upon it!'

'Miss Andrews, I fully intend that you should accompany Watson and myself. As you pointed out to my dear friend, your specialised knowledge could be of particular use to us in our search.'

'I am so relieved,' she sighed.

Holmes smiled politely, but avoided my glance.

'I should also like to see the papers you found in the cottage. I may be able to help you decipher them.'

'All in good time,' replied Holmes, briskly. 'For the present, I will ring for Mrs Hudson, our housekeeper, and she will see that you are comfortable for the night. In the meantime, I intend to pore over a few maps with an ounce of shag; and Watson, you had better get a good night's rest. I want you banging on the door of Cook's at nine in the morning to obtain our tickets of passage for Egypt.'

Ten

THE DECEIVERS DECEIVED

My head had barely touched the pillow before the refreshing vapours of sleep wrapped themselves around me. It was a deep, untroubled sleep without dreams. However, at some point, sweet, melancholic sounds seemed to filter through the mist of unconsciousness. Although faint, muffled even, they were persistent, willing me to take notice. Slowly, reluctantly, my tired brain teased and then roused me into wakefulness. I lay for some moments in the velvet darkness of my bedroom, still drugged by slumbers; and yet I was still aware of the sounds. It took me but a few moments, as reality forced itself upon my fatigued mind, before I comprehended what I was hearing. It was music: lilting, wistful music played on a violin.

Now fully awake, the explanation was simple: Holmes was keeping a melodic vigil. The music drifted like some mournful cry from our sitting-room below. On other occasions I would have turned on my side and surrendered my tired frame to sleep once again, but that night something pushed me into grabbing my dressing gown and slipping down to our sitting-room.

I entered quietly. The room was dimly lighted and Holmes was silhouetted against the window blind, his back towards me, his Stradivarius held delicately under his chin, the bow moving with slow, masterful ease across the strings.

As I closed the door behind me, the music stopped. Holmes froze. 'I hope my nocturnal recital has not kept you awake, old fellow,' he said softly, with genuine concern in his voice.

'Not at all.'

He spun around to face me with a broad grin. 'Good. A little Brahms is not only good for the soul, it is a lubricant to the thought processes. It helps one come to terms with realities, eventualities... the facts.' For a moment his face darkened, his brow furrowed, and I was no longer there: he was talking to himself. And then, as the sun emerged from behind a grey cloud, he flashed me another broad grin, placed his violin on the table, and bade me take my old chair by the fire.

'All is far from what it appears to be in this affair, Watson,' he said, sitting opposite me and leaning forward to stir the fading fire so that the embers glowed bright again for a moment, throwing his sharp features into amber relief. 'These are shifting sands. Indeed, they have shifted again this very day. We are surrounded by deceit and deceivers. Tricksters. From Setaph to...'

'I would like to hear.'

'For your account, no doubt.'

'So that you can share your burden,' I replied evenly.

'Oh, Watson, you are a good fellow. I sometimes undervalue your qualities.'

'Indeed, you do.'

Holmes gave a mirthless chuckle and murmured quietly, 'I am lost without my Boswell.'

He sat still for a moment, for all the world like a mannequin at

Madame Tussaud's; then, rubbing his hands together with a kind of sardonic glee, he sat back in his chair and began to tell me the remarkable truth concerning the Scroll of the Dead and those concerned with its discovery.

When I returned to my bedroom, my mind was in a whirl. It was as though I had been standing at a window watching a scene through thick net curtains, and now Sherlock Holmes, with his marvellous facility to expose the truth, had removed the curtains and cleared my view. As a result the scene was markedly different from the one I had perceived. Figures in my new landscape were revealed to possess different personas and motives. The implications of these revelations kept me awake for the rest of the night.

The next morning I breakfasted with Miss Andrews. Holmes was nowhere to be seen.

'He was up and out bright and early,' said Mrs Hudson in response to Miss Andrews' concern at my friend's absence. 'That's his way when he's on a case, isn't it, Doctor Watson?'

I nodded dumbly, swallowing a piece of toast.

'He did tell me that he'd be back at noon. Now is there anything else I can get you, my dear? More toast or another egg, perhaps?'

Miss Andrews shook her head.

When our landlady had retreated to her quarters, Miss Andrews rose from the table with a cry of frustration. 'Where has he gone? Why did he not tell us he had some business?'

I could not help but smile at the girl's naivety. 'Because that is the way he works. He is not given to confiding in people. He only lets others know what he wants them to know. I have worked with him for many years and yet he still keeps me in the dark until he considers the time right to illuminate my ignorance.'

My explanation did not erase the petulant look on her face. With a sigh of irritation, she strode to the window and gazed down into the street.

I glanced at my watch. 'It is nearly nine,' I announced. 'Time I was on my way to Cook's to book our passage. You will be safe here until my return. If you need anything, just ring for Mrs Hudson.'

The young woman parted the net curtain and leaned her forehead against the cool pane of glass. 'I shall be a good little girl, Doctor, and wait patiently for your return,' she said softly with neat sarcasm.

I have never felt comfortable when deceiving a woman, however essential the need. This occasion was no exception, despite Holmes' assurance that indeed it was absolutely essential. I was fully aware, as I left our lodgings like a skulking criminal, that Miss Andrews' gaze was on me. Dutifully, I hailed a cab and, acting out my charade, announced rather more loudly than I had intended that I wished to go to Cook's Travel Agents in the Strand. As we pulled away, I observed Skoyles, one of the Baker Street Irregulars, loitering casually across the street. He gave me a cheery wave.

When the cab reached Oxford Street, I leaned out and called up to the driver, issuing a a new set of instructions. He twisted his face into a scowl. 'Oh, so the 'oliday's orf then, eh?'

I nodded sheepishly.

Within half an hour, I had joined Holmes on the steps of the British Museum as arranged. Despite his sleepless night, he was fresh-faced. His eager, bright eyes shone with excitement and anticipation. I informed him of my breakfast conversation with Miss Andrews and he smiled broadly. 'It is so pleasurable to be in command of the stick which muddies their waters,' he cried, turning on his heel into the Museum.

Sir Charles Pargetter was surprised to see us so soon after our last encounter. 'I am truly sorry to interrupt your work again,' said my friend earnestly, 'but I do need further information before I can proceed any further with the matter of the stolen papyrus.'

The Egyptologist nodded and threw his hands out in an expansive gesture. 'My dear fellow, I am happy to be of assistance. I will tell you anything you need to know, if it will lead to the return of this precious artefact.'

'When the contents of the tomb discovered by George Faversham and Alistair Andrews were shipped to this country, did everything end up within the confines of the British Museum?'

'Most of the collection – yes.'

'But not all?' There was a sharp eagerness in Holmes' voice which caused Sir Charles to wrinkle his brow in a concerned fashion.

His response was carefully considered. 'Several items remained in Egypt; but these were of no historic interest to us. Faversham requested a few pieces to be kept in his own possession on the understanding that should the Museum wish to exhibit them it could.'

'What were those pieces?'

'I cannot remember the details of each item exactly. I have the full inventory in my files, but I do know that they were trivial artefacts – certainly by comparison to the mummy and precious items of jewellery.'

'Was one piece a Canopic jar?'

Sir Charles' eyes widened behind the pebble lens. 'Why, yes, I do believe it was. I remember it was a particular favourite of Sir George's. He made a special request to keep it.'

By the time Sir Charles had imparted this piece of information, Holmes had leapt from his seat and was halfway through the door. 'Thank you,' he cried, cheerfully. 'It is a confirmation I desperately needed.'

'What was all that about?' I asked in the cab as we returned to Baker Street.

'In breaking the code, I realised that a Canopic jar is central to this puzzle.'

'A Canopic jar?'

'...contains the dried organs of the deceased wrapped in linen. Henntawy's jar was a very interesting item: it was dog-headed and contained...'

When we alighted at Baker Street, Skoyles, who seemed to be in a devil of a hurry, rushed by us, bumped awkwardly into Holmes, and without a word of apology ran off down the street. Rather than appearing annoyed at this incident, my friend smiled: 'Good lad, that.'

Once in the hallway, Holmes held up a note in his gloved hand.

'From Skoyles,' I said, the dawn beginning to break.

'A subtle and yet effective means of passing information. That lad will go far.' Holmes scrutinised the note and gave a satisfied nod. 'Now, the next stage of the game must be played carefully. There is much at stake.'

'What do you want me to do?'

'Go upstairs. Assure Miss Andrews that our passage to Egypt is booked. Explain that I am still tying up the threads of another case before we depart. I'll leave the details to you. After all, creative fiction is your department.'

'What then?' I asked.

'Take tea with her and then invent a patient who requires your assistance.'

'Holmes...'

'And then,' he said quickly, ignoring my ejaculation, 'meet me in the snug bar of the The Prince Regent on Salisbury Street, near to the Conway Hotel, at eight o'clock sharp.'

'I don't suppose there is any point in asking why?'

'Astute as ever, Watson. Eight o'clock sharp, remember.' With that he slipped quietly out of the door and into Baker Street once more.

* * *

The Prince Regent was one of the less salubrious *rendezvous* in which I had waited for my friend. I arrived at fifteen minutes before the appointed hour to find the snug crammed with noisy drinkers, many of whom, judging by their abandoned demeanour, had been there some hours already. The air was so thick with tobacco smoke that it was almost impossible to see clearly across the room. With some difficulty, I made my way to the bar, squeezing past a knot of inebriated sailors who looked as though they were about to lose the power of standing upright at any minute. Eventually gaining a place at the counter, I managed to secure the barman's attention. I was just about to order a drink when a fellow pushed in at the side of me and called out brusquely, 'A pint of your best ale!'

I tugged the man's sleeve. 'You can get me the same, Hardcastle,' I called in his ear.

The Scotland Yarder turned in surprise. 'Doctor Watson! You're here already. Where's Mr Holmes?'

'I am here,' said a disembodied voice somewhere amidst the smoke-filled room. 'No time for drinks, gentlemen. We have a lady to surprise and a villain to apprehend.'

'What exactly is this all about, Mr Holmes?' enquired Hardcastle in a peevish manner, once we were out in the street. 'I had hoped to get home to the wife for a quiet supper together tonight.'

'I am sorry if I am responsible for rocking the boat of domestic bliss, Inspector, but I thought you would like to be present when two of the culprits involved in the Museum theft were apprehended,' replied my friend, with more than a hint of smugness in his voice.

Hardcastle tried to contain his surprise by coughing into his handkerchief. 'That's quick, even by your standards,' he said gruffly.

'You have your darbies with you?'

'I have. And a warrant as requested. But who is it we'll be nabbing?'

'All will be revealed in due course. Now, gentleman, we are about to enter the Conway Hotel. We shall spilt up and seat ourselves discreetly in the lobby. Read a newspaper or examine a menu, anything to blend into the background. Keep your eye on the reception desk and watch for my signal to move.'

The Conway was a modest hotel situated within half a mile of Charing Cross Station. Because of its close proximity to the railway, it was popular with visiting businessmen and theatricals. I had considered taking a room here myself when I first returned from India, but the rates had proved too expensive for a fellow with an income of but eleven shillings and sixpence a day.

We entered separately. The lobby was quite busy and there were very few seats available. I positioned myself by a pillar and picked up a copy of *The Westminster Gazette*, while Hardcastle seated himself behind a potted palm. Holmes sat at the writing desk apparently composing a letter. He was enjoying the moment, the subterfuge, and using us, the Scotland Yarder and myself, as puppets in his grand plan. Of course, I had some inkling of what was afoot, but certainly not the full details or ramifications of Holmes' plot. I comforted myself with this thought, for I knew that Hardcastle was completely in the dark. Holmes delighted in keeping the official police ignorant of events until the moment when he could surprise them with his brilliance.

Little did I know at the time that, while we waited and watched, we were also being watched. Somewhere in the shady recesses of the foyer, a tall blond-haired man with a plump white face and fiercely cruel eyes kept his own vigil while he smoked a series of Russian cigarettes. Like a Grand Master, he knew that, despite his protagonists' ruses, he was still in charge of the board.

* * *

We had not long to wait. Some twenty minutes after our arrival, as the crush in the lobby began to thin out, a young woman in a state of some agitation entered the hotel and hurried to the reception desk. From my vantage point, it was easy for me to observe that her face was flushed, while her brown eyes were wide with concern, and a thin sheen of perspiration covered her brow.

It was Catriona Andrews.

The three us watched from our different viewpoints as she made some urgent request of the desk clerk, who at length consulted his guest ledger and imparted the information that she so desperately desired. She then hurried towards the hotel lift. As she disappeared behind the clanging metal doors, Holmes was on his feet and making his own urgent enquiries of the desk clerk. With a dramatic gesture of his arm he beckoned us to him.

'201 is the room we require, gentlemen. We'll take the stairs, and that will give our charming client time to make herself at home.'

Wearing a puzzled expression, Hardcastle mouthed the word 'Client' to me, but Holmes, intercepting his query, announced curtly, 'Later, Inspector: full explanations later.'

I gave the policeman a sympathetic shrug.

Some moments later we stood in a brightly lighted corridor outside room 201. Holmes spoke to us in a whisper. 'It is unlikely that you will need your firearm, Watson, but I would be obliged if you have it on show in order to impress upon our friends that we mean business. Similarly, Hardcastle, have your handcuffs at the ready – you will certainly need them. Ready, gentlemen?'

We nodded gravely, whereupon Sherlock Holmes flung open the door of room 201.

The sight that met our eyes was indeed an extraordinary one. In the middle of the room were two figures: a man and a woman. They were holding each other in a close embrace. One of the figures was Catriona Andrews. The other was a man somewhat older than her. He was tall in stature with a waxy complexion and wispy grey hair.

At our sudden entrance they broke from each other's arms and turned to stare at us with looks of total amazement on their faces. On realising that her treachery had been discovered, Miss Andrews placed the back of her hand to her mouth to stifle a cry of horror.

Holmes stepped forward and bowed. 'Good evening. A touching scene indeed. Father and daughter reunited once more after the pain of separation. Let me introduce you, Inspector Hardcastle, to the happy couple over here: this is Miss Catriona Andrews, and this is her father, Sir Alistair, whom we had given up for lost.'

'You devil!' screamed the young woman. Within seconds her whole demeanour had changed. Having easily and quickly shaken off the emotions of shock and dismay, she took a step towards us, her body now consumed with fury and her face contorted with hate for my friend. She gave an unintelligible cry and flew at Holmes, her arms outstretched, her fingers curled like talons. Before he had a chance to defend himself, she was upon him, screaming, and clawing at his face. He fell back, helpless against such a ferocious attack from a woman. He seemed at a total loss as to how to react.

I rushed to the rescue and, with the help of her father, managed to pull the young woman away from my friend and restrain her. Incensed as she was, Miss Andrews possessed great strength, and it was some moments before we could release our hold of her safely. At first she struggled violently, ready to snap free and be at Holmes again, but her father begged her to be calm. He repeated his entreaties in a firm but soothing manner and eventually his daughter, recognising the futility of the situation, gradually controlled her anger. Her body relaxed and the ferocity gave way to tears. She fell sobbing into her father's arms.

Holmes was very shaken by the sudden attack. Awkwardly, he dragged a handkerchief from his pocket and mopped his brow. For a brief moment he had been jolted from his secure position of control and thrown into a situation that was totally unexpected. He stood now eyeing the crying girl strangely, his breath still emerging in irregular short bursts and his eyes flickering erratically, registering his total disquiet.

'You all right, Mr Holmes?' asked Hardcastle, placing a concerned hand on his shoulder.

My friend gave a stern nod of the head. His face was deathly white apart from a series of thin red scratches around the neck where the girl's nails had scored the flesh. Already blood was beginning to seep out of the deeper wounds. 'I suggest you arrange transport to Scotland Yard for these two,' he said to Hardcastle, his voice shaky at first and then resuming its natural authority, 'and afterwards, if you care to call round to Baker Street for a nightcap, I will furnish you with details concerning their involvement in the murder of Sir George Faversham.'

Eleven

SHERLOCK HOLMES EXPLAINS

'I will never understand women, Watson. They act without reason or logic. At all times their emotions, passionate and unthinking, rule their behaviour. Take the Andrews girl. One moment she is plotting some heinous crime with her father with heartless, clinical precision. However, on being discovered she flies into an unrestrained fury like a wild cat and then finally collapses in tears. Hah! Give me the cold, calculating, and controlled ruthlessness of Professor Moriarty any day. At least there was intellectual consideration behind *all* his actions! With women the unpredictable is all you are able to predict.' Sherlock Holmes paced up and down in an agitated manner as he loosed this tirade against womankind in general and Miss Catriona Andrews in particular.

We were back once more in our sitting-room at Baker Street and I had dressed the wounds the girl had inflicted upon my friend. They were minor hurts, but Holmes was more than irritated by having to surrender to my ministrations. He saw the girl's attack upon him as an affront to his dignity and perception. I knew that Holmes' anger was caused not so much by the 'emotional irrationality' of Catriona Andrews but more by his own failure to anticipate her actions. He did not like being unprepared in his dealings with people, and he had been completely unnerved by her assault.

I did not respond to this outburst, knowing that my best course of action was to assume the role of a silent witness. At length I gave a weary sigh of boredom which stopped my friend in mid-sentence. 'For goodness' sake,' I said gently, 'do sit down and have a pipeful of shag to calm your nerves.'

His eyes narrowed and he gave me a strange, accusative look; but he did as I suggested. For a time we both lapsed into silence; then, just as I was about to open up a discussion about the implications of the night's events, there was a discreet tap at our door and Hardcastle entered. He drew up a chair by the fire and joined us in a smoke.

'Now then, Mr Holmes, I would appreciate a full explanation of how Sir Alistair Andrews and his daughter are implicated in murder and the theft of that Egyptian papyrus. At present they are under arrest solely on your word, and if I am to keep my job I will need more than that.'

Holmes nodded and leaned back in his chair. 'Of course, my dear fellow,' he replied, in a voice which indicated that his equanimity was in the process of being restored. 'There are four people mixed up in this affair, four greedy people who are determined to locate Setaph's Scroll of the Dead. You have two of them in custody: Sir Alistair Andrews and his unscrupulous daughter. However, their full involvement in this business came some time after the theft of the Henntawy papyrus.'

'So who broke into the Museum and made away with it then?'

'Sebastian Melmoth and Tobias Felshaw.'

Hardcastle opened his mouth, as if he were about to question Holmes regarding the certainty of this assertion; and then shut it again as he thought better of it. He had learned, as I had, that it was foolish and pointless to question Holmes when he was in mid-flow.

'You know Melmoth and his little aristocratic friend, Felshaw, of course?'

Hardcastle nodded. 'Not personally, mind. We don't exactly move in the same circles, but we are aware of the strange couple at the Yard. I know they get up to some funny business, but I must say I hadn't pegged them for the type who would commit murder.'

'They are exactly that type,' replied Holmes coolly.

The inspector sucked on his pipe and frowned. 'But there's one little fly in your ointment: Melmoth is dead. He was killed in a shooting accident a few days ago.'

Holmes grinned. 'Never believe all you hear about that scoundrel. Rumours of his death are much exaggerated. Take it from me, Inspector, Sebastian Melmoth is very much alive. Indeed, for Melmoth and his crony, death is not an issue. They intend to rise above that particular rite of passage. Hence their urgent desire to get their hands on the Scroll of the Dead. They believe that it will give them a kind of immortality.'

'What nonsense!' exclaimed the policeman.

'Indeed, but Melmoth is convinced otherwise. Setaph's scriptures are his holy grail and salvation. He is prepared to kill to own the Scroll. For several years he has been searching, experimenting, reaching out into the realms of darkness to discover the way to conquer death. Recently he acquired what he really believed was the answer to his unholy prayers: a document which he thought would unlock the secrets of Henntawy's papyrus. Therefore, he became determined to get his clutches on it by fair means or foul. Inevitably, he chose the foul. With his acolyte, Felshaw, he stole the papyrus from the British Museum. The act of murder added zest to the exploit. He is that kind of man.'

Hardcastle inhaled noisily and shuddered. 'I had heard he was odd.'

'He is more than odd,' I said. 'He is evil.'

'However,' continued Holmes, 'after some study, I am now convinced that this "key" is worthless. It is merely a devious piece of nonsense created by Setaph himself to fool and mislead those who would discover his secret. Or to be more precise, those who lacked the appropriate wisdom and insight he deemed necessary to share his secret.'

Hardcastle scratched his head. 'Let me get this straight. You're saying that this key, as you call it, if it does exist, is a useless trick.'

'Exactly. It is a false trail set by Setaph for the unworthy.'

The policeman allowed himself a throaty chuckle. 'He was a tricky so and so, this Setaph, wasn't he?'

Holmes nodded. 'Now this is how I see the chain of events following the theft. Once Melmoth had both the key and Henntawy's papyrus in his possession, he believed it would be a simple matter to decipher the symbols and crack the code which would reveal the location of Setaph's magical Scroll of the Dead. Such was his arrogance. Of course, he was wrong. He was as much in the dark as ever. Not realising that the key document was useless, he sought expert help. He approached Sir George Faversham, who refused to help him. Sir George was desperate to locate the Scroll of the Dead for himself in order to beat his rival Andrews to it and earn himself a large entry in the history books. He was hardly likely to assist those two scoundrels in *their* pursuit of *his* goal. We cannot be sure if Faversham's death was premeditated or if it was the unpleasant outcome of the visit that Melmoth and Felshaw paid upon the old archaeologist. However, it is certainly clear to me that our two friends murdered Sir George Faversham and ransacked his house in order to make it appear as though a common burglary had occurred.'

'If what you say is true, that's two murders on their heads.'

'At least.' Holmes relit his pipe and beamed warmly. He was now in his element: explaining the complex details of a case to a captive audience. 'Our two antagonists then approached Sir Alistair Andrews for assistance. Sir Alistair Andrews was already involved with Melmoth and his crony. He was far less scrupulous than his fellow archaeologist, and no doubt he agreed to help them on the understanding that, once they had gleaned the requisite information from the Scroll of the Dead, he would be allowed to claim credit for discovering it. However, he was obviously having difficulty in deciphering the code, and that is why, in desperation, they approached Faversham for help.' It was Holmes' turn to chuckle now. 'And all the collected brainpower of Melmoth, Felshaw, Andrews, and his daughter still could not break the code set by a man over 2000 years ago. Of course, they were hindered somewhat by attempting to read the message by using the useless key, just as the wily Setaph had planned. His trickery reached over the centuries to block their malevolent plans. That's when they brought me into the matter.'

'They *brought* you in?'

'In a manner of speaking. Melmoth must have been be aware of my monograph on codes, and realised that I was probably the only man capable of breaking the one set by Setaph. In this instance, he was right. Disregarding the fraudulent key, I discovered that the real message concerning the location of the Scroll of the Dead was coded within another code in Henntawy's papyrus. I have come across this device only twice before, most notably in the case of the Vatican cameos. Interestingly enough, that was another instance where a priest proved to be skilful at deception.

'Our motley crew had to be very cunning and devious concerning the manner in which they secured my services. They knew that I would not respond kindly to an open request. Melmoth was shrewd enough to realise that I suspected him of the museum theft and the murder of the night watchman, so in order to prevent me from getting any closer to that particular truth, he organised his own death. He killed one of Felshaw's estate workers, damaging his face so that the poor man was unrecognisable. Felshaw presented the world with the shocking news that

Sebastian Melmoth had been involved in an unfortunate shooting accident and was dead, thus superficially blocking off one of my avenues of investigation. But they knew that while the world mourned his demise, I would not be fooled by this rather transparent ruse. They were sure that I would investigate and I was led, like an ass by the nose, to a cottage on the Felshaw estate in Norfolk, where sufficient clues were left for me to stumble upon, providing me with enough information to work on the code and Henntawy's papyrus. This I did. I approached the puzzle not as an Egyptologist but as a detective; and I solved the mystery.'

'You did?' Hardcastle beamed, sitting forward in his chair eagerly. 'You are a wonder, Mr Holmes, you really are. You say you know where this so-called Scroll of the Dead is located?'

Holmes gave him a brief smile. 'At least, I know where it *was*,' he replied quietly. 'But let me finish my tale in order, my friend, before we come on to the whereabouts of the magic Scroll. Having kindly cracked the code for Melmoth and company, they needed to know my findings, so they presented me with another mystery. This is where Miss Catriona Andrews came into the picture. She gave me sufficient information to lead me to deduce that her missing father had been abducted, the implication being that he was being forced to work on the papyrus for Melmoth. In engaging me to find Sir Alistair, she had a strong, legitimate reason for staying close by my side. They hoped to convince me that they had already broken the code and that I would hare after them in order to apprehend them at the site of Setaph's tomb somewhere in Egypt, when in reality they would be following *me* to learn of its location. Their grave error was assuming that the Scroll of the Dead was lodged somewhere in Egypt. It is not. It is in this country.'

'This country!' gasped the Scotland Yarder. 'Where?'

Holmes shot him a frosty glance. 'All in good time and proper order. They waited for me to make arrangements to travel to Egypt, receiving detailed reports of all my plans and movements from their spy in the camp, Miss Catriona Andrews. With the help of the Baker Street Irregulars, I soon located the hotel where the girl's father was in waiting. I sent her a telegram this evening, purporting to come from him, requesting her to meet him at the hotel at eight this evening. I couched the message in suitably dramatic terms, stating that the matter was most urgent. And thus we were able to nab two of our birds.'

'What about Melmoth and Felshaw?' I asked.

'They are shrewd fellows. No doubt they are already aware of the situation.'

'It's rather a complicated affair, Mr Holmes, and while I can only applaud your detective work up to now, it seems it does not get us much further down the road of apprehending the murderers and restoring Henntawy's papyrus to the British Museum.'

'Patience was never one of your virtues, my friend,' remarked Holmes languidly, stretching himself in the chair. 'I believe that within forty-eight hours, the other two birds will be in our net and the manuscript safely restored to the museum.'

'I am pleased to hear it. Then allow me return to an earlier question. Where is this blasted Scroll of the Dead?'

Twelve

A Visit To The Elms

Sherlock Holmes was enjoying himself too much simply to hand over the reins of the case to Hardcastle at this juncture. He had been happy enough to relate how he had reached his conclusions regarding the investigation so far, but he artfully deflected all the policeman's questions regarding the location of Setaph's Scroll of the Dead. I knew my friend believed that he had passed on sufficient information to enable the inspector to continue his own detective work without his assistance. As always, Holmes was determined to plough a solitary furrow. Once he had started an investigation, he became determined to be the one to bring it to a satisfactory conclusion.

'As I have already intimated,' Holmes announced firmly to silence the protesting inspector, 'I believe that within forty-eight hours I will have the Scroll in my possession and Melmoth and Felshaw will have been apprehended.'

'But this is police business!'

'Then be about it. I am not preventing you. But let me remind you, my friend, it was your good self who sought out my assistance in the first instance, and it was I who presented two of the quartet of malefactors on a plate for you this evening.' Holmes' stern expression softened as he tapped the Scotland Yarder on the knee. 'I am a lone hound. I work better that way. I now have a strong scent, and my quarry is near. I am not going to pass it over to a pack of professionals.'

Hardcastle rose stiffly to his feet. 'It's not right, Mr Holmes. It's not right; and no fancy words about lone hounds will make it so. You talk about a pack of professionals – well, yes, I am a professional and I'm proud of it. What you are doing – withholding information – is most *un*professional to my mind.' He made his way to the door but turned again to address my friend before leaving. 'I hope you change your mind about this, Mr Holmes. If you do, you know how to find me.' With these parting words, he shut the door fiercely and thumped his way down the stairs.

Holmes smiled gently and stirred the fading embers of our fire. 'He will get over it. Especially when Melmoth and Felshaw are behind bars and the British Museum has its precious papyrus back.'

'You believe that Sir George Faversham had Setaph's Scroll all the time, don't you?' I said.

Holmes gave a start and almost dropped the poker. 'Why, my dear Watson, this is wonderful. You have followed things marvellously.'

'I listened and observed. I have had years of practice.'

'Yes, yes, of course,' he said, grinning. 'I shall have to watch myself or you will be undermining my magician's art. Well done, Watson. I must say I am fascinated to learn how you reached this conclusion. Do tell me how you read the riddle. Let's see if there are any gaps.'

I smiled, pleased that I had surprised and impressed my friend with my statement in very much the same manner that he had amazed me on numerous occasions. 'Very well,' I said, lounging back in my chair. 'I cannot claim to have made any startling deductions, but the fact that you made enquiries about that dog-headed Canopic jar taken from the tomb of Queen Henntawy, and that Sir George Faversham had requested possession of it, was suggestive. Knowing of the devious mind of Setaph and that such jars are meant to contain a person's entrails, their essential body parts as it were, it would be fitting for this devious priest to secrete the Scroll of the Dead within the jar. How Sir George discovered this fact, I know not. I am also unclear why he did not announce his finding to the world, but kept it secret for many years. So you see, in essence, my knowledge is only slightly greater than Hardcastle's.'

'You do yourself a disservice, old fellow. Your gaps of knowledge are my gaps too. You are correct about Faversham. He discovered that the Scroll of the Dead was concealed in the jar by breaking the code in the papyrus found in Henntawy's tomb, as I did. The information is there if you know how to interpret it. Sir Alistair Andrews couldn't see it and indeed, still cannot see it, but Faversham must have approached the problem much in the same manner as myself: with a scientific eye rather than that of an archaeologist. Setaph knew that those who came after him seeking his magical text would assume it was hidden in his own secret tomb; so, to confound them, he placed it in the tomb of Queen Henntawy, secreted in the innocent Canopic jar. Faversham's request to take possession of a simple item like the jar would have seemed quite innocent to the authorities of the British Museum. Little did they know that he was holding the most precious relic from the whole expedition. As to why he kept his discovery of the Scroll of the Dead a secret, I cannot be sure. It is one of the missing pieces of the puzzle. It may be that Faversham had that peculiar passion which some collectors have. There are those who possess great works of art but keep them locked away in darkened rooms and never let anyone view them. The possession is all. It may have been the same with Faversham. One can imagine his delight at the frustration of his rival, Andrews, who was so desperate and determined to locate the very piece that Sir George kept in his own house.'

'Now he is dead, perhaps we shall never know.'

'As Melmoth would no doubt observe, the dead can tell us many things. Tomorrow we will visit Faversham's house in Kent in search of the truth.'

While Holmes and I were engaged in this conversation, Sir Alistair Andrews was lying on a bed of hard sacking in a cell in Scotland Yard. He had not yet been charged, but he knew that imprisonment and disgrace lay before him. His dream of fame and recognition as one of the world's greatest archaeologists had flaked into ashes within a matter of hours. He stared up at the barred window through which pale moonlight filtered, the only illumination the cell enjoyed. Tears moistened his eyes. And yet he was angry. Angry that he had been such a fool. Such a stupid, gullible fool! The anger grew within his breast like fire in a furnace. It burned inside him with a feverish intensity. He shifted his position on the bed as the discomfort grew, but there was no relief from it. He was wracked with self-loathing. He rolled over onto his back as his breathing grew more laboured. The pain grew. His chest felt so tight, it was as though it were being crushed by a great weight. And his heart... his heart pounded and pounded like an engine out of control, the vibrations reverberating in his ears, drowning out all other sounds. It seemed as if his heart was about to explode. He just managed to cry out for help before losing consciousness.

Sir George Faversham had lived at The Elms, a large house on the outskirts of Lee in Kent. Holmes had hired a dog cart from French and Barnard's, and he drove the seventeen or so miles himself. 'It is so much easier to spot if you are being followed in one of these these things than on a crowded train,' he explained. Most of our journey was spent in silence. It was a warm, bright day and it was fascinating to observe the changes of surroundings on our journey. Passing over the sluggish, leaden Thames, we left behind the heart of the great, grey city, encircled it seemed by a ring of smoking miasma, and drove through the rough, red-bricked wilderness of the outskirts before reaching the belt of pleasant suburban villas. It was not long then before we were cantering down leafy lanes where the crippling hand of man had not yet made its mark. Our journey to Lee caused us to touch on three English counties, starting in Middlesex, passing over an angle of Surrey, and ending in Kent. It was a delightful drive.

On the outskirts of Lee, Holmes reined the horse in to the side of the road to consult a map. Sir George Faversham's house, The Elms, lay at the north side of the town. Holmes stabbed at the map with a gloved finger. 'There we are, Watson, less than two miles away. We take the next road on the left.' So saying, he dropped the map at his feet and we set off again.

'I have not been able to glean much detail about Faversham apart from what Sir Charles could tell me,' announced Holmes as we trotted along in the bright sunshine. 'Apparently he was a bachelor who favoured a very private life. "Secretive and reclusive" were Sir Charles' words. He lived at The Elms with his secretary, John Phillips, and just one manservant, Dawson. The house is now up for sale. I contacted the land agent yesterday and arranged this visit. Dawson is expecting us and will show us around the property.'

'What about Phillips?'

Holmes gave a shrug of the shoulder. 'I have no notion as to his whereabouts. Most likely he is seeking another position. He may have already obtained one. Dawson will no doubt be able to furnish us with details.'

Following this brief interchange, Holmes lapsed into silence once more until we arrived at our destination.

The same bright sunshine that had favoured our sojourn to Kent filtered through the grimy windows of the prison infirmary. Pale yellow light, diminished by its journey through the gloomy ward, fell gently on the grey face of Sir Alistair Andrews, bathing it in a delicate amber hue. His daughter, Catriona, sat by his bed holding his hand, the blue veins rigid and clearly visible through the translucent skin. It was cold. It was colder to her than ice. It was colder than the fear that she now felt. It was colder than the hate that she was nurturing within her bosom. Her stare was fixed somewhere in the distance while her eyes brimmed with tears.

There was a rustling noise behind her and a nurse came forward and took her arm. 'Come along, my dear, I am afraid you must go back now.' She looked over her shoulder at the uniformed officer who stood some six feet away. He took a step forward as the nurse gently raised the girl to her feet. Catriona Andrews leaned forward and placed a kiss on her father's white forehead and then she was led away, first by the nurse and then by the officer, who took charge of her as they reached the door of the ward. For a moment the girl hesitated and turned again to gaze back at her father's bed. She was just in time to see the nurse pull the sheet up over his face.

The Elms was a grand structure. As we passed down a curved, lush, tree-lined drive, the house, as if by magic, suddenly swung into view. It stood before a large circular lawn, the borders of which were crammed with the bright hues of spring flowers. The building itself was of precise Georgian proportions, the smooth honey-coloured stone glowing in the morning sun. There was a clipped tracery of ivy around the main door, but apart from that the front of the building was unblemished.

As Holmes drew up beside the front portico, the large door opened and a short, grey-headed man emerged to greet us. His shoulders were stooped and he gazed out at us from large rheumy eyes. 'Good day, gentlemen,' he said, almost bowing. 'You are Mr Holmes and Mr Watson, I take it.'

'Indeed!' cried Holmes, jumping down from the cart and shaking the man's hand. 'And you must be Dawson.'

The man nodded deferentially. 'Please come in, gentlemen, I have been expecting you. You would, perhaps, care for some refreshment after your journey before I show you around the building.'

'Most kind,' said Holmes.

We entered the impressive hall with its shiny parquet floor and bright chandeliers. There were many artefacts denoting Sir George's fascination with Egypt placed around the spacious chamber: vivid masks of vibrant hues, various items of jewellery, an ancient map of the Nile basin displayed over the fireplace, and a large, brightly coloured sarcophagus standing on end at the foot of the broad staircase. However, to my surprise there were no signs of the recent burglary.

Holmes made this observation. Dawson appeared slightly unnerved at our knowledge of the crime – as though it placed some blight on his master's house. 'The blackguards were obviously common ruffians,' he replied. 'Apart from making a mess of a few rooms, they took very little with them. Thankfully, most of Sir George's collection remains intact.' He moved forward and placed a hand gently on the sarcophagus, stroking it as though it were a living animal. 'Of course you will appreciate, gentlemen, that Sir George's effects, his collection of Egyptian items, are not included in the sale of the house. They are to be removed to the British Museum in due course.'

'I fully appreciate that point,' returned Holmes, 'but having a fascination for Egypt and its history myself, I wonder if I can prevail upon you to include a tour of Sir George's fascinating collection as we view the house.'

'I do not see why not, sir. Now if you'll come this way and take a seat in the drawing room, I'll see to the tea.'

We took tea, and in our role as potential buyers we chatted to Dawson about the house and grounds and the nature of the local area. However,

Holmes, eager to start the tour, ignored the tea and quickly prompted our guide to start showing us around. It was an impressive building, one of the most attractive houses I had seen, and very large for a man with no wife or family.

'Sir George adored the space and freedom that The Elms gave him,' Dawson explained. 'He wasn't a gregarious man and he felt he could lose himself in the house if he wished, despite the fact that usually there was only myself and Mr Phillips, Sir George's secretary, on the premises.'

At one point on our tour we were shown what Dawson called the Egyptian Gallery, a long, dimly-lighted room which contained the nucleus of the Faversham collection. Holmes spent a great deal of time scrutinising the items closely, while I engaged Dawson in conversation to keep the fellow occupied. There were one or two empty cases, and other evidence of the recent break-in, but to my untutored eyes the collection appeared to be more or less intact. In my own examination of the items on display, I saw nothing that could be regarded as significant to our investigation, and certainly there was no sign of a dog-headed Canopic jar. From his bleak expression, it was clear that Holmes was similarly disappointed with his examination. He gave me a dismal shake of the head as we left the gallery, indicating that his search had been fruitless.

'What is this room?' queried Holmes some moments later, as we were being led back downstairs to the drawing-room. He stopped and pointed to a heavy green tapestry draped across a recess on the corridor wall. Before Dawson could respond to the question, my friend stepped forward and pulled back the tapestry to reveal a door. He tried the handle: it was locked.

Dawson frowned and appeared flustered. 'Oh, that is... er, was Sir George's private study.'

'A secret room, eh? Not easy to spot. I bet the burglars missed that. Well, we should like to see inside,' said Holmes sternly. 'If we are to consider buying a property, we need to see all aspects of it, all of its chambers.'

Dawson hesitated. 'No one was allowed in there, sir. Sir George kept it as a strictly private room.'

'But he is no longer with us,' I remarked softly.

Still the man hesitated. His loyalty to his master remained strong, even after death.

'Come, sir, the room...!' snapped my friend impatiently.

Slowly, with great reluctance, Dawson withdrew a key from his pocket, unlocked the door, and we entered. It was a small, claustrophobic room, made all the more so by the heavy velvet curtains which were draped across the window, allowing only a thin shaft of light to invade the darkness and spot the carpet with a sharp strip of illumination. Holmes strode forward and, pulling the curtains apart, flooded the room with bright sunshine. As he did so, my heart skipped a beat for I observed, standing by a large document-cluttered desk, a dog-headed ornament – surely it was the Canopic jar we were seeking. Holmes had seen it too, and with a nod and a raised eyebrow indicated that I should distract Dawson while he examined the item. With my hand on the manservant's arm, I drew him to the window and asked him to explain the location of the room in relation to the rest of the house. I kept feeding him with questions as best I could while at the same time keeping an eye on Holmes who, with great stealth, knelt down by the jar and raised the lid silently. His face looked stern as he peered inside. Then gingerly he placed his hand deep down into the jar. He withdrew it moments later and I could detect from his gloomy countenance that it was empty. Clearly the Scroll of the Dead was not there. Involuntarily, he gave a gasp of exasperation. Dawson instinctively turned at the sound to discover Sherlock Holmes examining the vast array of books on the shelf.

'If you gentlemen have seen enough... I would be happy if we could leave this room now. I am really not at ease in breaking Sir George's word, even though he is, as you say, no longer with us. I know it may seem foolish to you, gentlemen, but until his things have been packed away, I shall still continue to think of it as his private study.'

Holmes was about to concede to this entreaty when his eye fell upon something that caught his attention. It was a photograph on Sir George's desk. He picked up the silver frame, examined it, and then passed it to me. The photograph featured two men standing by a rowing boat at the edge of a stretch of water with a bank of trees as a backdrop. The older man had his arm around the younger one's shoulder in an avuncular fashion. Dawson stood by our side and, unbidden, explained the photograph. 'That is Sir George with Mr Phillips, his secretary. The photograph was taken with Sir George's own camera by one of the servants.'

'But I thought you were the only member of the household staff,' I said.

'At The Elms, yes. But there is Bates, the housekeeper at Grebe House.'

Holmes eyes lit up with excitement. 'Grebe House. Where is that?'

'It is Sir George's country retreat in the Lake District. It is situated on Grebe Isle, a small island on Ullswater. It suited Sir George's love of solitude and privacy.'

'Tell me,' said Holmes, his sense of excitement barely concealed, 'did your master keep various Egyptian artefacts up at Grebe House also?'

'I have no doubt he did, sir. But I have never visited it. In fact, to my knowledge, apart from Bates, the housekeeper who used to tend the house in his absence, Mr Phillips was the only other soul to have been allowed on the island. Sir George had no children himself, you see, and he rather regarded Mr Phillips almost as his adopted son. They were very close. Even when Sir George was buried he...'

'Where was he buried?'

'Sir George wished the location of his resting place to be kept a secret.'

'He was buried on the island, wasn't he? He was buried on Grebe Island.' Holmes stared fiercely at the retainer, willing him to reply to the statement.

At length, Dawson nodded dumbly. 'Yes, sir, according to his final wishes. Mr Phillips accompanied the coffin up to Grebe House only a few days ago...'

Thirteen

EN ROUTE

Within minutes of this revelation, Holmes and I were in the dog cart, heading back to London. Dawson had been surprised by our rather sudden and swift departure, but Holmes had assured him that we had seen enough of the house for our purposes and were favourably impressed. 'We will contact the land agent in due course regarding our decision,' my friend had informed him as we left.

'I do not feel proud for misleading the fellow,' Holmes told me as we rattled down the drive, 'but there are greater issues at stake here than a minor deception. I would have liked to warn him about Melmoth and Felshaw, for I am sure they will pick up our trail soon — if they have not already done so.'

'But surely they don't know what to look for. They are not aware that the Scroll of the Dead was secreted in the jar. Or are they?'

Holmes shook his head. 'No. If they did know, they would be ahead of us now. However, what they are sure of is that *we* are on the right trail, and therefore they must follow in our footsteps. All they need to do is ask Dawson to recount what he told us and they will soon deduce what our next move will be.'

'Which is, I presume, to travel up to Grebe Isle.'

'Of course,' Holmes grinned. 'That is our journey's end and will, I predict, be the setting for the final scene in this grim drama.'

'And what of Melmoth and Felshaw?'

'We do not have to worry too much about those two dark birds of a feather at present. We certainly shall not lose them. Strange, is it not, Watson? We are in a unique situation: this time the criminals are chasing us rather than the other way around.' My friend gave one of his strange little laughs and his eyes glittered with sardonic amusement. 'However, there will come a time when we shall be forced to renew our acquaintance with the recently deceased Mr Sebastian Melmoth and his rather nasty accomplice, Tobias Felshaw. It is a moment I look forward to with relish.'

While we were entering the city of London in the early afternoon, Dawson opened the main door of The Elms to two unexpected visitors. They were strangers to him. One of the men stepped forward, pushing Dawson unceremoniously back into the hall, while the other closed the door behind them. The more dominant of the two men was tall, with a round, pale face framed by long blond hair. He moved close to Dawson so that their faces were within inches of each other. The manservant caught the sweet aroma of a rich eau de cologne.

'I have certain questions to ask you,' the man said smoothly, his lips parting in a grin. Dawson had no difficulty in sensing the real menace in his voice. 'Answer them fully, correctly and without hesitation and...' the man paused, pursing his lips; then, dropping his voice to a whisper, he added, '...and then we may let you live.'

By that evening Holmes and I had caught a sleeper train from Euston and were travelling north to Penrith, the nearest mainline station to Ullswater.

'This is the last train until the morning, so with a bit of luck that should give us some eight hours' start on our friends,' he observed as we took our seats in an empty compartment.

'Unless, of course, they hire a special.'

Holmes' features darkened. 'Unless of course they hire a special,' he repeated glumly. It struck me that he had not contemplated such a possibility.

'What do you think is waiting for us on Grebe Isle?'

'It is hard to say. There are too many unknown aspects in this affair to be able to create a set of reliable logical suppositions. One thing is for certain, however: Sir George Faversham's interest in the Scroll of the Dead went beyond the simple passions of a collector.'

'What do you mean?'

'Did you note the books on the shelves in his study?'

'I saw that he had a large collection...?'

'The titles, man, did you not note the titles?'

'I cannot say that I did.'

'There was a whole section of learned and apocryphal tomes dealing with the mysteries of death and life after death. There were books on Spiritualism, vampirism, necromancy, reincarnation, and religious and philosophical tracts of many hues and persuasions, all dealing with the secret of death.'

I felt a chill hand clutch my heart as I glimpsed the unpleasant truth at which Holmes was hinting. 'You think that Faversham wanted the Scroll of the Dead for the same reason as Melmoth: to use it to... to raise the dead!'

'It would seem so. How such a brilliant archaeologist could be fooled into thinking that this ancient tract could really give him the secret of life over death – open the door to immortality – I do not know...'

'Obsession. Once a person fixes his mind on a certain goal or object he can become clinically obsessed. The victim is then blinkered against logic and sound reason; he sees only his goal. Melmoth has these characteristics too. Ironically, intelligent minds are more susceptible to the obsessive state.'

'Thank you, Doctor.' Holmes nodded and gave me a smile. 'Well, if we are correct about Faversham, it will explain why he kept his discovery of the Scroll of the Dead secret for so many years. It was not for its historical or its artistic qualities that he clasped it to his bosom. He saw it as a practical manual to escape the grave.'

'But he is dead.'

'But perhaps not yet in his grave. The Scroll was of no use to him while he was alive. But now...'

'What are you saying?'

Holmes leaned forward, closed his eyes, and pressed his long fingers to the bridge of his nose. 'I am not sure what I am saying, Watson, or to be more precise what I admit to saying – but the evidence seems to point in only one way.'

'Which is?'

'That Faversham entrusted his secretary, John Phillips, his "adopted" son, as Dawson termed him, to perform whatever ceremony the Scroll of the Dead dictates, using his corpse in order to raise him from the dead.'

'Great heavens, it's obscene!' I cried.

Holmes sighed wearily. 'Obscene and pathetic. Obsession, as you so astutely observed. Obsession without recourse to reason, logic, or morals. Wild, misdirected obsession.' Holmes sat back and gazed out at the night sky sprinkled with stars, mere pin pricks in the heavens, and sighed. 'It is one of those rare occasions, my friend, when I hope to goodness that my inferences are wrong.'

'Come in here, gentlemen, and I will see what I can do for you.'

The stationmaster closed the door behind the two young men, shutting out the noise of the busy station. He lit an oil lamp and consulted a large ledger, muttering to himself as he did so. 'A special to Penrith, you say?'

The two gentlemen made no reply.

The stationmaster ran his finger down the various columns in the book. 'Yes,' he said at last, smiling, 'I think that is possible. Yes, yes, that is certainly possible.'

I did not sleep very much that night. The sleeping quarters were cramped and cold and my mind was teeming with nightmare thoughts and images of coffins and reanimated corpses. As dawn was breaking, I dressed and stood in the corridor with an early morning pipe and watched a new day blossom over the northern countryside. Through the mist clouds seething in the gulleys and valleys, I caught glimpses of grey-sheeted water set against the backdrop of the undulating purple-tinted hills, dotted in their lower reaches with banks of trees. It was a wild and yet restful landscape, and watching it grow brighter by the minute as the sun rose above the distant mountains had a calming and restorative effect on me. So entranced was I by this passing vision of natural ruggedness and beauty that I failed to notice that Sherlock Holmes had joined me.

'"Therefore am I still/A lover of the meadows and the woods/And mountains; and all that we behold/From this green earth",' he intoned softly, and added by way of explanation, 'Wordsworth. This was his country: the land of hills and lakes.'

We stood in silence for some time, gazing out at the passing scenery as the train shuddered and rocked its way up a gradient. Then, with a swift change of mood, Holmes consulted his watch. 'We arrive in Penrith in just under an hour. Let us retire to the restaurant car for breakfast. I am not sure when we shall have the opportunity to eat again.'

After a full breakfast of ham and eggs, sausage, toast and coffee, Holmes spread out a map on the dining car table. 'As you can see,

Watson, Penrith lies at the northern tip of Ullswater. The main road runs down the western side of the lake but Grebe Isle – there – lies to the east. So to speed our journey we must approach it from the eastern side of the lake.' He pointed to a thin wavering line on the map which ran along the blue patch of water. 'Although quicker, this route will be more difficult to follow. It appears rather basic. I suspect these lines marked here are merely dirt tracks. However, to some extent this will be to our advantage. They will afford us greater cover should we need it.'

I scrutinised the map closely to familiarise myself with the locale. Ullswater is a long, straggly lake, looking not unlike a crooked stocking. Grebe Isle, no more than a black dot on the blue shading on the map, was situated towards the southern end where the lake was at its widest.

'There appears to be a small promontory here virtually opposite the island,' I observed, pinpointing the location with my knife.

'Yes, I suspect there will be a small jetty with boats used for access to the Isle.'

'If not, we shall be in trouble,' I grinned.

'Nonsense,' said Holmes, returning my grin. 'You can swim, can't you, Watson?'

Penrith is the old capital town of Cumberland, built of the local stone in the ninth century. On leaving the station, we could not help but be aware of its sense of history as we passed the rugged Lakeland buildings, many of which dated back to the sixteenth century, flinty monuments to the skill of their architects and builders.

The sky was blue but dotted with ragged grey clouds, and a sharp wind cut through the folds of our coats. Although a stranger to the town, Holmes strode out with purpose as though he knew exactly where he was going. 'We seek a livery stable, and the likeliest place to locate one is the market place.'

'How do you know that we are walking in the right direction?'

'No secret, my friend. I obtained directions from the guard while you were paying for our splendid breakfast.'

Indeed, it was not long before we located the little market place, which was bustling with activity. It was just after eight in the morning, and various shopkeepers were pulling up their blinds, opening their doors, wiping down their counters, and setting out their produce for the day. Workmen and businessmen criss-crossed the tiny square, hurrying to their places of employment. Holmes and I, moving at a slower pace, completed a circular tour but failed to spy out any livery stable. 'We shall have to make enquiries,' announced Holmes, and he led me to one corner of the square towards a small open-fronted shop, which bore the sign 'Joseph A. Cooper, Blacksmith' in black lettering above it.

'A blacksmith will certainly know where we can locate a couple of horses.'

Joseph A. Cooper, a brawny fellow with fiery side-whiskers which matched his shiny red face, fulfilled Sherlock Holmes' prediction. Still wielding a glowing horseshoe with a pair of long pincers, he broke off his task to provide us with the information we required. 'You want Flinty O'Toole – he's the best horse man round here, is old Flinty,' he told us brightly. 'He keeps a smallholding out towards Stocksbridge. It'll not be more'n a couple of mile out of town. Two fit gen'lemen like yourself can make it easy within the hour. Tell Flinty that Joe Cooper sent yer and he'll set you up with a couple of good nags.'

After he had given us detailed directions on how to reach O'Toole's smallholding, we thanked the blacksmith for his assistance and set off at a brisk pace. Soon we had left the environs of the town and were making our way along primitive country roads where the influence of the nineteenth century had not yet been felt. Joe Cooper was accurate in his estimations, for within forty minutes we had located Flinty O'Toole's place. He was a small Irishman with a pleasant demeanour, a leathery complexion, and bright, twinkling blue eyes. He soon fixed us up with a couple of fine mounts and half an hour later Holmes and I were riding along by the eastern shores of Ullswater.

That very morning, near the city of London, in a grey suburban churchyard, a small funeral was taking place. There were few mourners, but there was a discreet police presence. Standing some way back from the graveside was a non-uniformed sergeant and his superior, Inspector Amos Hardcastle.

As the coffin bearing the lifeless body of Sir Alistair Andrews was lowered into the dark maw of the grave, the young priest intoned: 'He that believeth in me shall have everlasting life.'

Catriona Andrews, her face covered by a dark veil, stooped over the grave, whispered some final words to her father before scattering a handful of earth onto his coffin. She then let out a wail of despair. It sounded like the howl of a wounded wild animal, and it cut harshly through the sepulchral silence of the graveyard. It was painful to hear her, and even the hearts of the waiting policemen were touched by the anguished cry. They bowed their heads in sympathy.

And then, suddenly, the girl was on her feet, and with the quickness of a greyhound was racing away through the graveyard, dodging in and out of the gravestones with great dexterity and speed. So sudden had been her flight that both Hardcastle and his sergeant were taken completely by surprise. For some moments they were caught in a kind of daze as they struggled to comprehend what they had seen. Then the inspector snapped into action, pulling the young sergeant with him. 'Come on, Porter. For God's sake, she mustn't escape,' he cried, haring off in the same direction as Catriona Andrews. The sergeant followed suit, unceremoniously leaping over the open grave, nearly knocking the stunned clergyman to the ground in the process.

But by now the girl had, it seemed, disappeared completely.

Had the purpose of our expedition not been such a dark and serious one, the ride we took along the shoreline of Ullswater would have been most refreshing and relaxing. It was good to be on a horse again. I had not ridden since my days in Afghanistan, and yet I felt at home in the saddle. One sees the world from a completely different and quite unique perspective from the back of a horse. In other circumstances I should have been very happy, but always at the back of my mind were thoughts about the unknown dangers which lay ahead. The sun may have been shining on the gentle rippling waters and the scenery may have been a blessing to the eye, but such things could not erase the growing sense of unease I felt. Not even Sherlock Holmes could be sure what we were likely to encounter when we reached our destination. Against this uncertainty, the soothing rhythm of a trotting horse and the beauty of nature had no power.

'It looks as if you will not have to swim after all,' cried Holmes, breaking my reverie. He pointed ahead to where a little wooden jetty reached out into the lake. Beached on the shore by this rickety structure were three green rowing boats.

I looked out across the lake and there, virtually adjacent to the jetty, I saw in the distance a dark shape rising out of the glistening water: Grebe Isle.

Flinty O'Toole was washing his hands by the pump when he sensed that he was being watched. A shadow fell across him. He glanced up and found himself facing a tall stranger with long blond hair. However, it was not the stranger's appearance that brought a chill of fear to his spine. It was the gun the man was pointing at his heart.

Fourteen

GREBE ISLAND

For some moments we stared out at the little island, a dark curved silhouette rising from the waters like the back of some great sea creature. From the shore it was impossible to make out any detailed features and there was no sign of habitation – certainly there was no smoke rising from any hidden chimney. It looked innocent enough in the spring sunshine, but I wondered what strange and diabolical secrets it held.

Dismounting, Holmes and I tethered our horses to the uprights of the jetty; then we set about dragging one of the ancient rowing boats into the shallows. Once the craft was bobbing on the water, Holmes stepped aboard, retrieved the oars from the bottom of the boat, and positioned himself as oarsman. I gave the prow, which was facing the shore, a heave in order to propel it out into the lake before clambering aboard myself.

With some difficulty, Sherlock Holmes manoeuvred the boat around in the direction of the island and then we set forth on our voyage. 'I am rather rusty, I am afraid,' my friend cried over the sound of the wind and the slap and splash of the oars. 'I haven't rowed since my university days.'

He tugged on both oars and after a time managed to build up a steady rhythm that sent the boat moving through the water on a reasonably steady course. A casual observer would have thought that he was a city gent out for a day's fun in the country. Certainly his demeanour betrayed nothing of any darker purpose behind our nautical excursion.

Out on the lake, any warmth generated by the pale yellow sunshine we had enjoyed on the shore was dissipated, and the sharp wind that knifed its way across the waters cut through our clothing with a chilling force. I wrapped my coat more tightly around me to little effect and shivered as the wind buffeted our little vessel. The island was over half a mile out from the shore and it was indeed tiny. Holmes pulled mightily on the oars and we made good progress. As we drew nearer I finally caught sight of Grebe House through a screen of trees. It appeared to be a strange, circular building of mock Gothic design, with dark stained-glass windows glinting back at us like huge winking eyes.

'What exactly is our plan of action?' I called to my companion, who seemed completely absorbed in his task of rowing.

'The situation is too serious for subterfuge,' he replied. 'We must remember that Faversham's secretary, Phillips, is not a criminal. As I see the matter, he has no connection with the theft of the papyrus or any of the murders. He is merely a misguided man carrying out the instructions of an employer he undoubtedly loved and respected. We must face him with the truth – unpleasant though it may be. We need also to inform him that he is our bait for bigger fish.'

'I just hope that Phillips has not performed some atrocity on the dead body of his master.'

'It would be unfortunate, but whatever he has done, it would have been carried out as an act of devotion, not desecration. However, his state of mind may be disturbed, and it would be as well to have your pistol handy just in case he reacts violently to our intrusion.'

My hand closed around the butt of my old service revolver in my pocket. The feel of cold hard metal gave me a comforting reassurance.

Soon we were approaching the jetty of Grebe Isle, the twin to the one on shore. Holmes allowed the boat to glide forward at the last minute until it lodged itself with a crunch in the shingle. We secured it to one of the wooden uprights of the jetty and scrambled on to *terra firma* once more.

Grebe House was situated some hundred yards from the shore in a saucer-like dip which, with the aid of the trees and a wild, neglected garden, made it virtually impossible to see from the shore of the lake. It looked starkly out of place in the lush green environment of the isle. Its blackened stone and ornate carvings reminded me of a small church in the city rather than a country house. There was a large, incongruous, wooden outbuilding attached to the side of the house.

Without a word, we made our way up the pebble path which led us to a substantial oak door. Holmes tried the handle, but the door did not budge. It was locked. 'It appears that we shall have to make our visit very formal,' he observed, tugging vigourously on the large bell. We heard distant clanging in the depths of the house, but it roused no response. Holmes persevered with the bell for nearly a minute and then resorted to hammering on the door.

We waited, listening intently, but the only sounds we could hear were the thrashing of the foliage in the breeze-blown trees and the occasional cry of a bird.

'Perhaps there is no one in there,' I said at length.

'Oh, yes, Watson, there is someone in there. I am convinced of it. I just hope the fool has the sense to let us in,' Holmes muttered impatiently. He pulled the bell again while I battered the door with my fist. At last we heard a sound from inside. It was muffled and faint at first and sounded like footsteps. They appeared to be approaching the door in a slow, slithery fashion and then suddenly they stopped. There was a brief silence which was followed by the grating noise of a key turning in the lock. Instinctively my fingers clutched the handle of my gun.

Slowly, the oak door opened wide. Standing before us, holding a lighted candlestick in one trembling hand, was a young, dark-haired man. I recognised him from the photograph I had seen at The Elms. It was the person we had come to see: John Phillips, Sir George Faversham's secretary. But it was a shock to observe the change that had been wrought on the appearance of his youthful features. There were premature streaks of grey in the hair which hung lankly around his gaunt, white, unshaven face. Lustreless eyes, dark-rimmed through lack of sleep, stared at us in a wild, furtive, haunted fashion. His mouth hung open, the lips moist with saliva. The fellow's whole appearance, with stooped shoulders and shuffling gait, was that of an old man.

He stared at us for some moments, his mouth working silently as though he was on the verge of uttering something, but had either forgotten what it was that he was about to say or was unsure of how to phrase it. In fact it was Holmes who spoke first.

'Mr Phillips, I am Sherlock Holmes, and this is my associate Doctor Watson. We have come here to help you.'

'No!' cried the young man suddenly with a snarling ferocity, his whole frame shaking now with a feverish animation and his eyes bulging in their sockets. 'No! You must go. You are disturbing my important work.' With a clumsy motion he attempted to close the door on us, but Holmes stepped forward, preventing him. Taking hold of the handle, my friend forced the door wide open and pressed forward so that Phillips, thus challenged, had no other recourse but to step back into the house.

'You either see us now and we help you,' my friend announced with cold authority, 'or we shall have no alternative but to inform the authorities that you have stolen property on these premises and that you are indulging in unnatural and un-Christian practices with the dead.'

Phillips's mouth gaped and he retreated further into the gloom of the hallway. 'Oh, my God,' he groaned, his eyes rolling wildly. In a daze, he staggered backwards, his free arm flailing, reaching out for some means of support. He found none. Still stumbling, he lost his balance and crashed to the floor in a swoon; the candlestick, released from his grasp, skated off into the darkness.

I rushed forward and knelt at his side, taking his wrist to test his pulse. It was feeble and sluggish. 'This man is barely alive,' I said as Holmes joined me at his side.

'Is it exhaustion or are there other symptoms?' he asked, kneeling down and cradling the young man's head in his arms. He prised back the flaccid eyelids but only the blood-veined whites were visible.

With Holmes' assistance, I removed Phillips's jacket and examined his arms for signs of injections. I wondered whether his exhaustive state was due to drugs, but the skin was smooth and unblemished.

'It is a type of exhaustion,' I said at last. 'Probably enhanced by nervous tension. His features and manic behaviour suggest that he is not a strong person, physically or mentally. If we get him somewhere warm and find a reviving drink – brandy perhaps – he should regain consciousness.'

To my surprise, Holmes jumped to his feet and shook his head. 'No. Leave him where he is. This is a splendid opportunity for us to examine these premises without hindrance.'

It was typical of Sherlock Holmes to place the considerations of the investigation before the welfare of a sick man – albeit a sadly misguided one. However, in this instance I saw his point. Phillips was in no real danger and his exhausted condition did provide us with such an opportunity. By the light from the open doorway, I spied a chaise longue at the far end of the hall. I suggested we move Phillips there so that at least he would be resting comfortably. Holmes agreed and we carried out the task.

Picking up the candlestick, he lit it again. 'Obviously, there is no gas or electricity on the island, so this simple stick of wax will be our prime source of illumination. Let us explore.'

And so we began a tour of that weird, round house. While the sun shone outside the building, we moved around in almost pitch darkness inside. I managed to locate another candlestick to aid us. There were also the dull-coloured glowing spots of light from the occasional stained-glass window, but these were feeble aids in a house that somehow seemed to revel in its own interior blackness.

We discovered that all the rooms were on the ground floor: the staircase merely led to a gallery around the dome of the building. There was a simple kitchen, dining-room, sitting-room and three bedrooms, all of which were Spartan and provided nothing of special interest to our investigation. Then we came to what was obviously Sir George's study. It was crammed with various Egyptian artefacts, including yet another brightly gilded sarcophagus set up on end on the back wall of the room. Holmes seemed particularly interested in this. Whipping out his lens he examined it closely.

'You don't think it contains Faversham's body, do you?' I asked.

'I doubt it, Watson. However, it is interesting to note that this sarcophagus only dates back to the early Victorian period.'

'What!'

'It is a copy only a little better than those used in side shows to fool the gullible public. Here, take my candle.'

I did as he asked, and with both hands he began to prise the lid open. It swung wide with ease.

'Modern hinges,' Holmes observed with a wry smile, 'so much more effective than those old Egyptian ones.'

What was revealed when the lid was opened was a great surprise to me: there was no base to the sarcophagus. It was, in all essentials, a door, a cunningly concealed door, which I could see, as I moved forward with the candlesticks, led to a descending flight of steps. 'A hidden cellar!' I exclaimed.

'*Au contraire*, my dear Watson. The term cellar is far too mundane a description for what lies beneath our feet. This staircase surely leads down to Faversham's secret tomb.'

I shuddered at these words.

'Come, let us discover if my deduction is correct.'

Taking one of the candlesticks from me, Holmes led the way through the sarcophagus door and we began to descend the narrow stone staircase. The steps curved round in a spiral and were illuminated at intervals by flickering oil lamps set into recesses in the wall at shoulder height. Using a habit I had picked up from Holmes, I counted the steps; there were twenty-eight. As we descended, I could not rid myself of the impression that we were leaving behind the real world of rationality and sense and entering a strange, pagan one of dark menaces and madness.

At the bottom of the staircase we found ourselves in a low-ceilinged chamber lit by four tall braziers, their rich vacillating flames and smoky tendrils casting eerie, dancing shadows onto the plaster walls. As Holmes had intimated, the chamber was indeed a replica of an Egyptian tomb. The walls were decorated with drawings, bright paintings, and tapestries from that mystic bygone age. At the far end of the tomb there appeared to be a small altar, holding a series of earthenware dishes containing various coloured liquids and, at the centre, a small golden casket. Hanging behind the altar was a large tapestry which covered the whole of the rear wall. It was blue in colour and featured images in bright yellow: a bird with a human head hovering over a mummy.

'Like the Egyptians he studied and admired all his life, Sir George Faversham prepared for his death in their fashion,' observed Holmes soberly. 'Note the wall paintings depicting characters important in the transitional stage between life and death. There is Anubis, the jackal-headed god; see also Osiris, god of the dead; and there is our old friend the ibis-headed scribe of the gods, Thoth.'

I could not concentrate fully on Holmes' words, for my attention was caught by the structure placed in the centre of the tomb. It was a large, stone, open casket, decorated around the side with carvings of animal and birds and stacks of corn. Inside the casket lay the body of a naked man. He seemed to be packed, like some dead animal, in what at first glance appeared to be moss, but which, on closer inspection, I saw was a bed of fine green crystals.

Holmes held his candle over the corpse. 'Sir George Faversham,' he said softly. As the flame flickered erratically, throwing small shifting shadows into the casket, it appeared as though the body was moving, stirring uneasily as if waking from a deep sleep. I shuddered at the concept of this rebirth.

'He has been treated to the embalmer's art,' said my friend in a voice strained with emotion. 'The body is packed in natron salt to purify and preserve it, and then,' he pointed to the vivid scars etched across the stomach area, 'the intestines are removed – as is the case here. The brain is usually removed last by a vicious process of pulling it down portion by portion through the broken sinus.'

'Great heavens, it's revolting!'

'By the appearance of the skull it would appear that Sir George has so far escaped that indignity.'

'But how on earth could anyone rationalise this barbaric treatment with the idea of conquering death? The removal of the entrails and the brain – how could a man function after having been butchered like that? It is beyond logic.'

'Magic *is* beyond logic, Watson. Obviously, Setaph failed in his task to bring the dead to life, but I think he believed that he could preserve the spirit of that person – the *ba* as the Egyptians termed it, represented there on the large tapestry as the bird with the human head. So preserved, the *ba* could then find another form of existence – another host perhaps. To ensure that this transition could be brought about, the traditional embalming ceremony was a necessary procedure.'

'So Phillips has done all this?'

'Yes, I have.'

We both spun round at this statement to see the gaunt figure and pallid features of John Phillips standing at the foot of the stairs. With faltering, uneasy steps he came towards us and gazed down at the body of his master in the casket, his hands clinging onto the sides as though for support.

'I begged him to see sense,' he said. 'I begged him to acknowledge that Setaph's words were the writings of a bitter man who had failed in his quest to conquer death. I told him that the Scroll of the Dead was just a desperate rigmarole of mumbo jumbo, an arcane camouflage to cover up Setaph's failure.' Phillips shook his head vigourously. 'But no, Sir George would not listen. He really believed that whatever was done to the body, the earthly shell, held no consequence as long as the spirit survived. This could then inhabit some other shell and rise as though from a dream to a new life.'

Tears were now rolling down the young man's face and his frame shuddered with emotion. Holmes and I remained silent, allowing Phillips the opportunity to release himself of the awful burden under which he was suffering.

'He made me promise to carry out the ceremony exactly as laid down by Setaph in his accursed Scroll. What could I do? I loved him. These were his beliefs and I could not betray his trust... I could not break my promise, even though I knew I was desecrating his body. Even though... At least he died in hope...'

I felt only sympathy for this young man who had been driven by his devotion and love for his misguided master to carry out the most awful acts of sacrilege on the body of the man he cared for most in the world. The selfless courage to accede to Sir George's requests was remarkable, and it was no wonder that the fellow was now a broken man.

'I... I am glad you have arrived, gentlemen,' he continued. 'Your presence now prevents me from going further with this monstrous ceremony. I welcome your constraint.' He gave a nervous little giggle and then with the sleeve of his coat wiped a thin trail of saliva from his chin. 'Do with me what you will.'

'Where is the Scroll of the Dead?' asked Holmes briskly.

With faltering movements, as though in a trance, Phillips made his way to the far end of the chamber where the altar stood. From the small golden casket there he pulled out a series of ragged yellow documents and held them out to us with shaking hands, tears welling in his eyes. 'Behold, gentlemen,' he said, 'here is the cause of this calamity. Here is the Scroll of the Dead.'

'Splendid,' cried a voice behind us. 'I arrive at a most opportune moment.'

At the sound of this new, yet familiar, voice, I turned to face the pale, malevolent features of Sebastian Melmoth. He stood at the bottom of the staircase with a gun in his hand and a wide grin on his face.

Fifteen

THE CHASE

Melmoth moved further into the chamber and, as he did so, his accomplice, Tobias Felshaw, emerged from the shadows of the staircase behind him. Felshaw, a thin, arrogant smile grazing his lips, was clutching a small leather bag in one hand and a gun in the other.

'Well, gentlemen, this is all rather cosy,' announced Melmoth expansively, in unctuous tones. His apparent pleasant behaviour only thinly disguised his true nature.

'"Journeys end in lovers meeting", eh, Mr Holmes? And yet you do not seem surprised to see me.'

'Indeed, I am not surprised,' my friend responded evenly. 'However, I had expected you earlier.'

Melmoth's grin broadened. 'I assure you that I did intend to be here earlier, but you know how unreliable those special trains can be. Still, it would seem that the timing of our arrival has been most opportune. Mr Phillips, I observe that you hold in your hand the *raison d'être* for my visit.' Suddenly the smile vanished and the features darkened. 'Now, sir, if you would be so kind as to pass me the Scroll of the Dead.'

Phillips, his mind further addled by the sudden arrival of these two strangers, stood still, staring blankly at the intruders. 'Who are you?' he asked in a quiet voice.

'I am afraid, sir, that we have not the time, nor have I the inclination, for such niceties.' The eyes glittered with menace. 'Now hand over the Scroll.'

Phillips still did not move. It was clear to me that his failure to comply with Melmoth's demands was prompted more by a sense of bewilderment than defiance.

'The Scroll,' reiterated our adversary, intense irritation showing clearly in his voice.

'Why?' asked Phillips.

'Because I have a gun and you do not,' snapped Melmoth, suddenly firing his pistol in anger, the bullet just missing Phillips's head. The sound of the shot filled the low chamber, reverberating like theatrical thunder. Felshaw moved forward and snatched the papyrus documents from the dazed secretary's limp grasp and placed them in the leather bag. He then pushed Phillips down to the floor and struck him a cowardly blow with the butt of his pistol. The young man stumbled back against the altar with a cry of pain, but he retained consciousness.

'You devil!' I cried, stepping forward in an effort to aid the injured man.

'Stop where you are!' barked Melmoth, cocking his pistol and aiming it at me. 'Do not be foolish, Doctor. This is no time for futile heroics.'

'Foolish!' I cried out in anger. 'You are the one who is foolish, Melmoth. You are the one who is prepared to kill and injure innocent people as you so desire just to get your hands on a few faded leaves of useless papyrus.'

'I assure you that these "few faded leaves", as you call them, are beyond price. They open a dark door to a new life – a life that is not circumscribed by death.'

'You really *are* a fool, Melmoth, if you believe that. Look at Sir George

Faversham.' I pointed to the corpse in the stone casket. 'There is no life there. He is just a dead man whose body has been mutilated in the course of Setaph's ceremonies.'

Melmoth had not registered fully the presence of the grim figure in the casket and, on seeing it properly for the first time, his face blanched. Felshaw, too, seemed unnerved at the sight of the scarred and bloodied cadaver, and took a step back.

'The intestines have been removed,' I continued. 'How can there be rebirth when vital organs are missing? This corpse will never rise up and enjoy a new life.'

'Of course not,' Melmoth replied at length, his composure restored. 'The full process has not been carried out. His *ba* has not been saved. And now, of course, it never will be. It is for others to reap the benefit of Setaph's secret.'

'Watson is right,' interjected Holmes quietly. 'Look at the mutilation. Are you prepared to risk that? Is your belief in this ancient document so strong that you will undergo such butchery in search of an uncertain truth?'

Melmoth gazed once more at the corpse in the casket. The sight seemed to both fascinate and horrify him, so much so that he failed to respond to my friend's taunt.

'If you really believe those yellowing scraps of papyrus can bring you a kind of immortality,' continued Holmes, 'then you are not merely foolish: you are mad.'

'Madness is objective, my dear sir. How are we, mere mortals, qualified to judge who is mad or sane? We play with insignificant arbitrary measures which in a thousand years may prove the reverse of the current beliefs – and neither judgement is likely to be correct. True madness is genius, and that is the path which I follow. Death is not the end; it is merely a transition to something better, something more wonderful. I am the ardent seeker of that age-old truth, one that the ancient sages knew but which has been lost to the modem world. However, Mr Holmes, I am sensible and realistic enough to realise that it would be foolish, reckless, to take risks needlessly. Let us say that we will experiment first before subjecting ourselves to this ultimate test. Others will be given the opportunity to pass through that magic door to the wonderful life after death before we indulge ourselves.'

'More murders.'

'Giving a new life is not murder, Mr Holmes, it is a blessing.'

Felshaw crossed to his friend and tugged at his sleeve. 'Let's go, Seb, don't waste words on these worms. We have what we came for, let's not delay.'

'Words of wisdom as usual, my dear Toby. What would I do without you?' So saying, he planted a small kiss on Felshaw's forehead. 'Very well, gentlemen, we must take our leave of you. Please do not attempt to follow us. There will be little point. We have wrecked all the boats by the jetty apart from one and we shall avail ourselves of that vessel for our escape. Come, Toby.'

On reaching the bottom of the staircase, Melmoth turned to face us again, his eyes shining brightly. He addressed Holmes in a soft, almost whispered tone. 'You came very close, Mr Holmes, very close. But not, I am afraid, close enough.' With a wave of his hand he retreated up the stairs in a languid fashion as though, now in possession of Setaph's scroll, the sense of desperation and urgency which had controlled his thoughts and actions for so long had dissolved, washed away by his triumph. The search for his own personal Holy Grail was over and the beatific grin which lit his features revealed clearly how he was savouring the moment. Felshaw followed him, moving backwards, his gun trained on us until he disappeared around the curve of the staircase. Whipping out my revolver, I made to follow after them but, as I did so, Felshaw threw down one of the oil lamps which were used to illuminate the staircase. It crashed down into the tomb, smashing on the stone floor. The spill of oil and flames shot out like greedy yellow tendrils, immediately catching hold of some of the hanging tapestries. Within seconds they were alight and rippling with waving tongues of fire. Two more lamps were hurled down, adding to the growing conflagration.

In no time at all black, choking smoke began to build up in the cellar and fierce heat lapped around us as the fire spread. Soon the staircase exit was a bright curtain of impenetrable, searing orange flame. My heart sank. We were trapped in the blazing chamber.

Phillips staggered forward and gripped Holmes' arm. 'There is another way out,' he cried, gagging on the smoke. 'A secret way. Help me.' He dragged Holmes to the rear wall of the tomb behind the altar and began tugging hard at the large tapestry which covered the whole of the wall and had been secured to the brickwork. Holmes joined him in his endeavours and I rushed forward to assist them.

I was conscious of the fire roaring and growing in power behind us. As I tugged with all my might at the tapestry, my forehead was awash with perspiration. The tomb now had the intensity of an oven and the voracious flames spat and crackled as they advanced upon us. I glanced back briefly and saw through the fiery haze the body of Sir George Faversham, lying in the open sarcophagus, beginning to darken and roast. I turned away: it was a sickening sight.

With one unified tug from all three of us, the tapestry finally came down to reveal the entrance to a tunnel. It was about three feet in height.

'Sir George had this specially built. He had a terror of being trapped in the tomb,' cried Phillips above the roar of the flames. 'It's perfectly safe. It leads to an outbuilding.'

'I applaud his foresight,' said Holmes, as he pushed Phillips down into the tunnel. I followed next and Holmes brought up the rear, just as the sea of fire began to lap around the entrance. We had to crawl on our hands and knees, but at least for the first twenty yards or so we were able see our surroundings because of the faint yellow light radiating from the conflagration we had left behind at the mouth of the tunnel. Eventually, as the secret passageway turned and twisted and then ascended slowly, we slipped into complete darkness. It was indeed a strange experience, crawling on one's hands and knees in a black void with the only sensations being the touch of the rough, damp floor and the disembodied sound of the laboured breathing of my companions; it was a claustrophobic one also, with the narrow walls and low ceiling somehow strangely tangible and oppressive in the pitch dark.

We moved like automatons in silence. Our progress was steady but slow. Smoke was already billowing up the passageway as though the fire were using it as a chimney. We increased our efforts but had to stop from time to time for Phillips to rest and build up energy for the next stage. In reality it only took us some two or three minutes to reach the other end but at the time, in that blindfold-thick, smoky blackness, it seemed like hours.

Eventually the passage flattened out again, and shortly we came upon a vertical shaft. A dim light filtered down from above, illuminating a wooden ladder fixed to the wall of the shaft. This time Holmes went first, and he clambered with alacrity up the ladder. Within moments he was hauling Phillips and myself through a trap door up into a large wooden outbuilding. Holmes and I rushed to the window and observed Felshaw and Melmoth approaching the jetty. Obviously, having disposed of us, or so they thought, in their arrogance they now saw no necessity to hurry from the scene. They strolled to the shore as if they were taking a constitutional in St James's Park.

'Quick Holmes. If we run after them...'

'They are too far away,' came the quick response. 'They would be out on the lake before we reached them, and we have no boat in which to pursue them!' He banged the flat of his hand against the wall with frustration.

'What about this, gentlemen?' yelled Phillips, heaving a tarpaulin from a structure at the far end of the building. The tarpaulin fell away to reveal a strange-looking craft having the general outline of a large canoe.

'What on earth is it?' I exclaimed, as we both ran to examine it.

Phillips beamed. It was as though our dramatic adventure had shaken him from his malaise. 'It is a life-sized replica of Queen Henntawy's funeral barge.'

'Thank you so much, Aunt Emilia,' said Catriona Andrews, as she took the proffered cup of tea. 'It is so kind of you to accommodate me for a few days while father is away on business. I am very grateful to you for taking me in when I arrived in such a distressed state, and without any luggage.'

'Think nothing of it, my dear. I do urge you to see a doctor about the state of your nerves, however. You need a tonic or potion to help you relax.'

'I assure you that I am feeling much better now, Aunt.' Catriona attempted a weak smile as if to prove her assertion.

The old lady peered at her niece through a lorgnette. Examining the pale, drawn features and troubled eyes of the young woman, along with her crumpled and muddy clothing, she was far from being convinced that the girl was 'feeling fine'. However, she smiled sweetly and offered Catriona a muffin.

'This building was Sir George's workshop, and this boat was his pride and joy,' John Phillips told us with renewed vigour. 'It took him more than two years to build. He based its construction on the original plans found in Henntawy's tomb.'

I studied the strange vessel. It was some nine or ten feet in length and four feet across at the widest point, with two decorative fan-like structures at either end which curved over like the toe of a gigantic Persian slipper. It was not dissimilar in appearance to an Italian gondola, but I must confess that it appeared far less robust. Unlike the gondola, you could not step down into it because the deck was laid like a platform across the top of the boat.

'Will it float?' I asked.

'It has not been tested. Sir George wanted to complete painting the requisite symbols on the barge before trying it out on the lake.' Phillips indicated a half-completed frieze of golden images painted on the side. 'However, the Egyptians had no difficulty in sailing such vessels.'

Holmes tapped the hull. 'Papyrus construction?'

'Indeed,' said our companion, who by now had regained most of his composure and actually seemed to be enjoying himself.

'Well, Watson,' said Holmes evenly, 'are you game for a little trip on the lake?'

It was with comparative ease that Holmes and I lifted the craft from the stocks on which it rested and carried it towards the large double doors at the rear of the workshop. The lightness of the boat increased my unspoken misgivings about its reliability on water. These thoughts were caught by Holmes. 'Well, it *is* made out of paper,' he observed with a wry grin.

Collecting two spoon-shaped paddles from a rack on the wall, Phillips rushed ahead of us and threw open the double doors through which we progressed into the sunshine once more. As we headed towards the jetty, we caught sight of Melmoth and Felshaw in their rowing boat some fifty yards from the island. They appeared to be deep in animated conversation, while Felshaw struggled with the oars. They were oblivious of our actions.

'We may yet give our friends the surprise of their lives,' grinned my friend.

Then came the launching procedure. With some temerity Holmes and

Phillips, each grasping one of the fan-like appendages at either end of this strange craft, lowered it into the water. For a moment it rocked and bobbed uncertainly, knocking against the struts of the jetty and then, miraculously, it stabilised.

'These paddles propel the vessel along and we handle them as we would do with an ordinary canoe,' explained Phillips, 'but because of the barge's construction we have to kneel on the deck, resting on our haunches in order to manipulate them.'

It was quickly agreed that Phillips and I would man the paddles, while Holmes, a better shot than I, would stand in the prow ready to use his gun if the occasion arose. One by one we boarded this untried craft. As we did so, water momentarily spilled over the deck and the whole boat bobbed unnervingly as it settled deeper into the water. It had the erratic buoyancy of a cork. Once aboard there was only a three or four inch gap between the level of the water as it slapped around the sides, and the level of the deck.

I settled back on my haunches and grasped my paddle in readiness.

'*Bon voyage*,' cried Phillips, and struck the water with his paddle. I followed suit. The boat rocked and then with surprising smoothness shot forward in the water. I found to my great surprise that it was remarkably easy to manoeuvre, and within moments I felt a growing confidence in our voyage, so much so that I afforded myself a glance back at the island. I saw that the flames had already reached the ground floor of that strange round house: the windows, once dark, now blazed yellow with the fiery contagion. It would not be long before the building surrendered to the fire and the Egyptian treasures and mysteries housed there would be lost for all time. Sadly I turned away and shook these thoughts from my mind. At present there were more pressing matters.

I was not the only one to observe this fiery destruction. However, Melmoth had turned also to witness his handiwork. He was too far away as yet for me to distinguish his features clearly, but I could see from his stiffened body and upraised hand that he had observed us following in his wake.

Holmes gave a barking laugh. 'I came very close, Mr Melmoth, and I am going to come even closer still,' he announced cheerfully.

Melmoth was yelling something at Felshaw, who was in command of the oars. At first the young baronet froze as he stared, no doubt in great surprise, in our direction, and then he galvanised himself into action, pulling on the oars with all his might. It was clear to me that, despite his Herculean struggles, he was far from being accomplished in the art of rowing. The vessel jerked erratically, dragged about by the uneven strokes of the oars. I estimated that our antagonists were only some four to five hundred yards from the mainland, but we were fast approaching them.

'I think the best plan is for us to reach the shore before our friends, and then we can provide a very nice welcoming party for them,' said Holmes.

'It is possible,' cried Phillips. 'The speed of this vessel is amazing. Sir George would have been so proud.'

By now we were quite close to Melmoth's boat. I could see him hunched in the stern, his face clouded with wrath, his arm outstretched, aiming a revolver at us.

'Pull away,' cried Holmes, 'don't get too close.'

As he spoke, a bullet whistled past my ear.

Felshaw, dropping his oars momentarily, joined his companion and fired also.

This time one of the bullets hit the side of the boat. There was a dull thud and the whole craft dipped momentarily and them righted itself. I leaned over the side and observed a scorched hole the size of a sovereign. It was on the waterline, and as the boat rocked to and fro so the aperture dipped beneath the waves, allowing water to spill into the hull. 'Any more shots like that and we may not make the shore,' I yelled. I had only just uttered these words when another volley of shots rang out. Luckily they hit the water, wide of their mark.

'We must return fire,' cried Holmes. Kneeling down, he steadied his gun and fired. The bullet struck Felshaw in the right shoulder. He gave a wild cry of agony, and clutching the wound fell sideways, tipping the rowing boat violently. With an inarticulate cry of fury, Melmoth fired two desperate shots at us. The reports echoed over the choppy waters of the lake but the bullets flew past us without harm. Melmoth's next shot was more accurate. The bullet ripped through the side of the hull. At first the damage did not seem serious, but then it became obvious that we were slowing down and the barge had become more difficult to manoeuvre. Then I noticed that we had started to list slowly, while water gradually began to cover the deck.

By now Felshaw had managed to pull himself to his feet and, while clutching his shoulder, he fired at us once more, calling out some oath at the same time. The wind whipped his words away but the bullet caught Phillips in the leg. He gave a howl of pain and fell forward onto the deck and then began to slide overboard. Quickly slapping my oar down, I grabbed his coat and hauled him firmly to the centre of the deck, where he lay face down in a daze.

Holmes returned fire once more. This time it was Melmoth who was wounded when a bullet caught him in the left arm. He emitted an agonised bleat and staggered back, falling over the seat and hitting his head on the prow of the boat. In a desperate attempt to reach his friend, Felshaw overbalanced and toppled into the water. Within seconds he was floundering, thrashing wildly, his mouth agape in frenzied cries. It was clear that he could not swim. Like a drunken man, Melmoth pulled himself to his feet, obviously still somewhat stunned, and reached out from the side of the boat. He stretched his right arm towards his companion, but the fellow was so frightened that he could not respond. Snatching up an oar, Melmoth proffered this as a means of pulling Felshaw back onto the boat. It was within a few feet of him but now Felshaw was completely hysterical, screaming in panic and desperation. His arms flailed frantically as his head disappeared briefly under the murky waters.

As we watched this grotesque pantomime, our boat had begun to sink. The hull was slowly filling up with water and already the deck was slipping beneath the waves.

However, Sebastian Melmoth had lost all interest in us; his whole attention was focused on his drowning companion. He cried to him, waving the oar ever nearer the desperate man, instructing him to take hold of it, but Felshaw was now incapable of acting rationally. Total panic had frozen his mental capacities and all he could do was thrash about in the water, howling like a frightened child. Once again Felshaw's head, his mouth agape in terror, sank beneath the surface of the lake. This time it did not reappear.

Melmoth gave a roar of despair and jumped overboard in a wild attempt to reach his companion, but Felshaw failed to resurface. Melmoth splashed around in desperation, calling out his friend's name. There was no answer. The cold, placid depths of Ullswater had claimed a victim.

Now our deck was virtually submerged and I paddled furiously for the shore. Water lapped around Phillips' head as he lay face down on the deck and this returned him to consciousness. He sat up and shook his head to clear his brain, and although his face was pinched with the pain of his wound, he bravely reached for his paddle to resume his duties. But it was too late, for as he did so the main body of the boat dropped below the water level and began to turn on its side.

'Jump for it,' yelled Holmes, and he leapt into the water as the prow began to disappear into the lake. Grabbing hold of Phillips' arm, I pulled him with me into the icy waves. The freezing water was a jolt to my system and I gasped for breath. Briefly my head slipped under water, but I held on to my charge and very soon Holmes came to my aid. Between us we helped Phillips make it to the shore some fifty yards away.

Minutes later we staggered onto the shingle, dragging our companion with us. Despite the cold, and our clothes being heavy with water, Holmes and I were none the worse for our swim. I turned my attention to Phillips. The young man was still conscious but appeared badly dazed. We hauled him up into a sitting position and I examined his injured leg. It was little more than a flesh wound and there would be no permanent damage. Once this fact was established, I joined Holmes, who had walked back to the water's edge. He was staring out onto the lake at the little rowing boat. Melmoth had finally abandoned his search for his drowned confederate and was climbing back on board. He stood for some moments staring back at us and then began to row the boat.

'What is he doing?' I asked, as I realised that he was rowing away from the shore, back to the island.

Sixteen

THE GREATEST ADVENTURE
OF THEM ALL

Holmes did not reply to my question, but stared with furrowed brows out onto the lake.

'What is he doing?' I repeated, as Melmoth's boat began to gain momentum, retreating from the shore.

'I am not sure, Watson. His plans are in disarray and therefore he is not thinking logically. We shall have to follow him to find out.'

Within moments Holmes and I had dragged one of the remaining green rowing boats from under the jetty and were headed out into the lake, once more following in the wake of our adversary, Sebastian Melmoth. In the distance the silhouette of Grebe Isle shimmered strangely. Streaks of black smoke rose like dark fingers into the afternoon sky. At the heart of the dense rolling clouds, one could glimpse bright yellow flashes of flame – the heart of the inferno. It was clear that Grebe House was being consumed by the fire and no doubt the contagion would soon spread to the outbuildings and beyond, even to the water's edge. The island now held no benefits as a haven or bolt hole for Melmoth. I said as much to Holmes.

He nodded. 'He knows full well that he has no real means of escape, so I fear he is about to make some grand symbolic gesture.'

I stared ahead of us at the dark outline of Melmoth's boat and then realised that it was stationary. Having reached the centre of the lake, he had ceased rowing.

He was waiting for us.

Slowly, with gentle, even strokes of the oars, Holmes brought our boat within a few yards of Melmoth's. At our approach, he stood up shakily and turned to face us. His features were drawn and haggard. Gone was the silky smooth countenance, and certainly there was no trace of the beatific, triumphant smile I had seen earlier that day; they had been replaced by a mask of frustrated anger and incipient madness. However, the eyes, now hooded, still flashed with arrogance and disdain. In one hand he clutched the leather bag containing the Scroll of the Dead and in the other he held his pistol. Fresh blood glistened on the sleeve of his coat from the wound that Holmes had inflicted upon him, but as Melmoth gazed at us over that short stretch of water, this did not seem to concern him.

'Come no further, gentlemen,' he cried, his voice strangely flat and unemotional. 'Pray, please keep your distance, and then we can keep this meeting... amicable.' He pointed his gun directly at my friend.

'I believe that the time has arrived when it would be most prudent and sensible to apply cold hard reason to your thinking, Melmoth,' said Holmes, standing in the prow of our boat. 'Give yourself up now without any trouble and hand me the Scroll of the Dead. To act otherwise would be pointless.'

Melmoth smiled darkly and considered Holmes' words. 'Cold, hard reason. Yes, that was always your strength, Sherlock Holmes – and your weakness. Reason shuts out the improbable, the impossible. It is fine for solving crimes but so restrictive in solving life's greater mysteries. Reason does not allow one to dream dreams and to search beyond the known.

However, I must admit that I should have heeded the warnings that I was given concerning your involvement in this affair. I really should have left you alone. But the idea so appealed to me, you see. To have the greatest champion of law and order working for me without knowing it was such a delicious concept, I just could not resist it. Mr Sherlock Holmes, the famous consulting detective, would solve the mystery for me: the malefactor in this case. The inversion was so attractive. My little fancy, however, was my undoing: with your brilliant detective brain you discovered my deception. As a result my plans, my dreams, my aspirations are as ashes in the grate because of your damned "cold, hard reason". And because of you the only person I've ever loved is lying at the bottom of this accursed lake.'

'He lies there because of you,' Holmes replied simply. 'In playing the game of murder, death is often the forfeit one has to pay.'

'Oh, I intend to pay the forfeit. But first I have another duty to perform.' With a sudden movement, he swung his left arm in a circular motion with all his might and then released the leather bag. It flew high in the air and then dropped with a soft splash into the lake. It sank immediately.

He gave a coarse, bitter laugh before addressing us once more. 'I am consigning the Scroll of the Dead back to the hidden darkness where it belongs,' he crowed.

'A selfish gesture,' observed Holmes with remarkable restraint.

'Oh, certainly, but I feel I am allowed some selfishness at this moment – a moment when I am at last ready to set forth on the greatest adventure of them all.'

With slow deliberation, he placed the barrel of the pistol into his mouth and pulled the trigger.

The shot echoed across the silent waters of the lake.

Epilogue

Pawnbroker Archie Woodcock smiled to himself as the young woman entered his shop. She had been vacillating on the pavement outside for some ten minutes. He had begun to take bets with himself as to whether she would pluck up sufficient courage to enter. Now here she was standing before his counter. He had seen her type before. A middle-class lady who, for whatever reason, had fallen on hard times. They hated the idea of having to resort to a pawnbroker in order to secure necessary funds. It was not just the loss of an item, but also a symbol of their slide into poverty. Inevitably, whatever they pawned had great sentimental value, be it a ring, a necklace, a silver photograph frame, or some other personal trinket. Archie Woodcock wondered what item this pretty young lady in the shabby green velvet dress would offer him.

'Now then, my dear, how can I help you?' he enquired in his most ingratiating voice, leaning on the counter.

'You have a gun in the window,' came the firm, confident reply. 'I should like to buy it.'

* * *

Inspector Hardcastle was not pleased with Sherlock Holmes. He wore a sullen, ill-tempered look and his mouth was turned down in an angry grimace. 'You should have kept me informed,' he growled, as he sat opposite us in our Baker Street rooms two days after our adventure in the Lake District. However, it was clear to me that the Scotland Yarder's bluster was merely a thin disguise for a fit of personal pique at not being involved in the action, thus robbing him of the opportunity of claiming some of the credit for the effective outcome of the case. Indeed, for Sherlock Holmes the investigation had reached a reasonably successful conclusion. The Cumberland police had managed to fish the two bodies out of the lake and then dispatch them to the morgue at Scotland Yard: so, as Holmes had predicted, Hardcastle had his two villains and the hangman had been spared two jobs. On Holmes' advice, the police had searched Melmoth's town house and found Henntawy's papyrus stolen from the British Museum, and this had now been returned to a delighted Sir Charles Pargetter.

'But you lost the Scroll of the Dead,' moaned the policeman.

'Not exactly,' said Holmes. 'I know where it is located – at the bottom of Ullswater – but I appreciate that it is irretrievable.'

'Exactly, Mr Holmes. Irretrievable is the word.'

'A fact which, I must admit, pleases me.'

'What!' cried Hardcastle, a flush of indignation colouring his cheeks.

'It was an evil piece of work, written by an evil man; a mendacious document, designed to fool those misguided and corrupt souls who wish to cheat death. It is best left in the black mud at the bottom of the lake.'

'That's as maybe, Mr Holmes...'

'Oh, for goodness sake, Hardcastle, don't look so miserable. You have your men and the purloined papyrus has been recovered.'

For a moment, the policeman stared fiercely at my friend; then his features softened and he managed to give Holmes a brief smile. 'In some ways I suppose you're right,' he said with a sigh of resignation. 'And I must admit that I do owe you a debt of gratitude for your efforts...'

'It's very nice of you to say so,' cried Holmes, rubbing his hands together. 'Watson and I are always ready to spring to the aid of Scotland Yard.'

'Unfortunately,' said the policeman, his features darkening again, 'I cannot close the case just yet. There is one piece of the puzzle missing.'

'Oh?'

'Miss Catriona Andrews.'

It was early that evening when I received the summons. Holmes and I had just finished one of Mrs Hudson's special meals and were relaxing by the fire. Our landlady always felt it incumbent upon her to provide us with a sumptuous repast when we had been away from Baker Street for more than a day. It was as though she did not trust us to eat properly once we were out of her purview. Holmes, as always, ate sparingly, but I consumed the meal with relish.

'We must go away more often,' I joked, throwing my napkin down and easing my chair away from the table.

'I do not think that you can afford to put on more weight, old fellow. I need you lithe and fit. A week of Mrs Hudson's treats would soon have you waddling, rather than racing, after villains.'

As we finished the last of the wine, the conversation turned to our recent adventure and its consequences. 'It is rather sad,' observed my friend, 'when two essentially decent people like Sir Alistair and his daughter go to the bad. They have been corrupted by their own selfish greed, that vicious mole of nature. "His virtues else, be they as pure as grace, As infinite as man may undergo, Shall in the general censure take corruption from that particular fault".'

'Do you think Hardcastle will catch up with the Andrews girl?'

'Oh, yes. She is not a practised criminal. There are no permanent bolt holes for her. I am sure that within a month, if not sooner, she will be back in police custody. That is a fairly bleak prospect for her, I am afraid.'

'I believe you feel sorry for the girl,' I said.

Holmes pursed his lips and sighed. 'I believe I do, Watson, I believe I do.'

At that moment there was a gentle tap at the door and Mrs Hudson entered. 'There's a message for you, Doctor Watson. A young messenger delivered it just now.'

'For me?' I said with some surprise, taking the note and reading it. 'Ah, it's from Thurston, my billiards partner. He wants me to join him at the club tonight for what he calls rather cryptically "a very special game".'

'I should go Watson: it will help you relax after the strains and labours of our last few days. And a trip to the club will help tremendously in walking off the effects of Mrs Hudson's splendid spread.'

Our landlady gave a chuckle and began clearing the table.

'I think you are right, Holmes, about helping me to relax at least. I shall go.'

Leaving Holmes poring over some old case notes, I set off for my club at eight, unaware at the time that my departure was being observed.

The evening was pleasantly warm, so I followed Holmes' suggestion and walked to the club. Some twenty minutes later I checked in and made enquiries about Thurston. The porter informed me that my friend had not been seen at the club for several days. However, there was a message for me from another gentleman who was not a member. He handed me a sealed envelope which bore my name, written in a long, fluid hand. It was handwriting that I recognised instantly. The message was from Sherlock Holmes!

* * *

The clock had just struck a quarter-past-eight when the door of the sitting room of 221B Baker Street opened silently and a shadowy figure stood on the threshold of the room. Sherlock Holmes had the gas burning low and was reading a sheaf of papers with the aid of an oil lamp placed on a nearby table.

The figure, a vague dark silhouette, stood some moments observing the detective, who, wrapped up in his reading, had apparently failed to notice the arrival of his stealthy visitor.

And then without looking up from his studies he spoke softly, addressing the intruder. 'Close the door, my dear, and take a seat by the fire.'

With slow, deliberate movements Catriona Andrews did as she was bidden.

Holmes dropped his papers and turned to stare at the white-faced woman who sat on the edge of the chair opposite him. 'I have been expecting you,' he said quietly. 'I observed you this afternoon from my window. You passed by the door some three times. Your intention to call was clear, but you obviously decided that it would be better made under the cloak of darkness – and when I was alone. That message for Watson was patently a false one designed...'

'Yes, yes,' snapped Miss Andrews. 'I am not interested in your deductions. I have not come here to listen to those. I have another purpose.'

'Revenge.'

She nodded. 'I have come to kill you,' she announced simply, pulling a revolver from her reticule and pointing it at the detective.

'I cannot help thinking that your animosity is misplaced, Miss Andrews. You no doubt blame me for the death of your father.'

'No doubt. Certainly *I* have no doubt.'

'But is that rational? Does not the blame lie with you?'

The idea so surprised the girl that she failed to respond.

'Shouldn't you have prevented your father from becoming involved with Sebastian Melmoth in the first place? Sir Alistair was a respected and able archaeologist. Could you not see that he was risking his reputation, his freedom, and his life in falling in with that malefactor? The dream, the fevered desire to discover Setaph's Scroll of the Dead had overwhelmed his better judgements, but you – *you* could be more objective about it. *You* were not blinded by the same passion. *You* knew of the dangers. *You* knew that what he planned, what he agreed to, was wrong. *You* could have warned him. *You* should have stopped him.' Holmes' voice was forceful, passionate even, but now he paused and added simply and quietly: 'But *you* did not.'

'I tried at first,' the girl snapped, 'but he wouldn't listen. His desire was all-consuming. It was like a disease, a pain that needed relieving. He saw Melmoth's offer as his last chance. In the end I could not deny him that. If I had, he would have shut me out of his life, and I could not have borne that. I loved him, you see – loved him with all my heart and soul.' She tossed her head angrily, her eyes now wet with tears. 'But you... you wouldn't understand that, would you? Love. You can't make a deduction about love. Love cannot be analysed, placed under the microscope, or written up in a notebook. What do you know of the real world, with real people and real passions, Mr Sherlock Holmes? You just sit here in your dry and dusty room working on clues and theories, never considering the hurt, anguish, and tragedy in which your cases are soaked. People are merely pieces of the puzzle to you, like figures on a chessboard. As long as the mystery is solved you have no consideration of how their lives are affected by your actions. You do not care.'

Holmes was startled at this attack upon him. 'You may be right,' he said at length. 'I have little experience of emotional passions – love as you term it. It is too irrational for my taste. But I have understanding and empathy and I am well aware that you are suffering under a great burden of guilt. Guilt which you are trying to place upon me. But it won't work, Miss Andrews, because your basic honesty and decency tell you that it is wrong. I am a detective. My task is to track down wrongdoers. You and your father were involved in criminal activities. I tracked you down. Where is the blame in that? The fault lies with your father and yourself. And if your father could not be persuaded to act otherwise, as you say, then that relieves you of the blame, too, and the fault lies solely with him.'

The girl gave a bitter laugh and rose, moving backwards to the door. 'You make it sound so plausible, Mr Sherlock Holmes, so reasonable, like one of your deductions. But, as you have said, passion lacks reason and my passion is revenge.' She held the gun at arm's length and prepared to fire.

Hurriedly I read Holmes' note and fled from the club. It was striking a quarter-to-nine as I hailed a hansom and ordered the cabbie to fly like the wind to 221B Baker Street.

'Killing me will not solve anything, Miss Andrews,' said Holmes, his voice remaining calm and reasonable despite the fact that a revolver was aimed at his heart. 'Construct for yourself a version of events following my death. You have no safe haven to which you can return. Scotland Yard is close on your heels and it is only a matter of time before you are recaptured, but this time murder will be added to your crimes. How does that help you or your father? Certainly the world will fail to understand your need or your reason to kill me in revenge. Your death sentence would be assured. The whole scheme is madness. Put down the gun and give yourself up and face what punishment is due to you with a dignity and fortitude that would make your father proud of you. Then you can begin to make a new life for yourself. That is the best course of action. I am sure it is what your father would have wanted.'

Catriona Andrews moved closer to the detective, her features clouded with mixed emotions, and for a moment the gun wavered in her hand and she began to lower it to her side. Then suddenly anger flashed in her eyes and she raised the gun again. With a trembling hand she aimed it at Holmes once more. This time she cocked the trigger. The sound seemed to fill the whole room.

On entering 221B I crept up the stairs as quickly as I could, and listened at our sitting-room door where I could hear a female voice raised in anger. Stealthily, I opened the door.

'Whatever happens to me – and quite simply I don't care now – I will at least be content in the knowledge that I've put a bullet through the heart of Mr Sherlock Holmes.' Catriona Andrews' finger began to squeeze the trigger.

'Ah,' cried Holmes with a smile, glancing beyond the young woman to the shadows by the open door, 'Watson, old fellow, splendid timing as always.'

My friend's outburst disconcerted the young woman sufficiently to make her hesitate. On impulse, she turned round just as I made a flying rugby tackle for her, bringing her tumbling to the ground. As she hit the floor of our sitting-room, the gun went off with a deafening report and the bullet lodged itself in the plasterwork of the ceiling.

Holmes gave a heavy sigh and poured out two large brandies. 'After this evening's adventures, I think we both deserve a substantial reward,' he said, handing me a glass and sitting opposite me by our fire. It was some two hours after my timely return to Baker Street. In the intervening period we had had to deal with Mrs Hudson's frantic enquiries about the gunshot and then suffer her tirade about firearms practice in our sitting room, which was followed by the arrival of Hardcastle and two constables to escort Miss Andrews to the Yard. Mercifully, she went quietly and without a word. Holmes had made no mention of her murderous attack upon him and had already placed the young woman's gun in his little museum, out of sight.

'If the truth be known, Holmes, I am more than a little angry with you,' said I gruffly, after taking a sip of brandy.

Holmes affected an air of mild surprise. 'Oh? Why is that, my dear fellow?'

'Firstly, for not taking me into your full confidence from the start. You knew that young woman would call this evening and that she may well have posed a threat to your life...'

'Indeed I did. It was clear to me that she was the author of the note purporting to come from Thurston. She wanted you out of the way so that she could deal with me alone. But she would not have ventured in if you had been around, or skulking in the shadows waiting to pounce. You know how badly you do these things. I had to be alone – with no hint of a trap or subterfuge. I also did not want to place you in a position of risk or danger.'

'But you arranged for a message to be delivered at the club explaining everything.'

Holmes nodded smugly.

'But what if I hadn't arrived in time?'

'I knew I could keep her talking, and I have complete confidence in your alacrity.'

'A minute later and you would have been dead,' I snapped, still angry. 'Did you stop to think of how I might feel if I had failed? If you were shot it would have been your fault for being overconfident and arrogant – but I would have been left to shoulder the guilt. You never think beyond yourself.'

Holmes bowed his head and stared into his drink for a moment, before looking me straight in the eye. 'You are not the first person to make that observation this evening. I humbly beg your pardon, my dear Watson. You are quite right in that I had not considered the possibility of you failing me.' He smiled. 'You see, you never have, and I have come to rely upon that.'

I could not help but smile in response. 'That is all very well, but I beg you in future not to be so reckless, and to include me in your plans.'

'I shall endeavour to do so.'

We sat for some moments in silence. I was pleased that the air had been cleared, although I was under no illusion that Holmes would act any differently in future. His brilliant independence of mind and action was both his genius and his weakness, and was an innate part of his personality. To change this would be to change the man, and I certainly had no desire to do that.

'What do you think will become of Catriona Andrews?' I said at length.

'With a good counsel and a plea for mitigating circumstances of diminished responsibility, I do not believe the lady will languish for long at Her Majesty's Pleasure. Once she has got over her father's death, she will need to rebuild her life which, as a bright, forceful young woman, I am certain she will do.'

'If she does, she will be the sole survivor of this sad business.'

'Indeed. This case has been peopled with individuals who have sought to conquer or cheat death, and now the grim reaper has them in his thrall. Life presents sufficient challenges and pleasures without the need to delve into that particular mystery. It comes all too soon as it is. "To everything there is a season, and a time to every purpose under heaven. A time to be born and a time to die".'

So saying, my friend turned and stared into the bright yellow flames of our fire.

Also Available

the further adventures of SHERLOCK HOLMES

THE VEILED DETECTIVE

by

DAVID STUART DAVIES

AFGHANISTAN,
THE EVENING OF 27 JUNE 1880

The full moon hovered like a spectral observer over the British camp. The faint cries of the dying and wounded were carried by the warm night breeze out into the arid wastes beyond. John Walker staggered out of the hospital tent, his face begrimed with dried blood and sweat. For a moment he threw his head back and stared at the wide expanse of starless sky as if seeking an answer, an explanation. He had just lost another of his comrades. There were now at least six wounded men whom he had failed to save. He was losing count. And, by God, what was the point of counting in such small numbers anyway? Hundreds of British soldiers had died that day, slaughtered by the Afghan warriors. They had been outnumbered, outflanked and routed by the forces of Ayub Khan in that fatal battle at Maiwand. These cunning tribesmen had truly rubbed the Union Jack into the desert dust. Nearly a third of the company had fallen. It was only the reluctance of the Afghans to carry out further carnage that had prevented the British troops from being completely annihilated. Ayub Khan had his victory. He had made his point. Let the survivors report the news of his invincibility.

For the British, a ragged retreat was the only option. They withdrew into the desert, to lick their wounds and then to limp back to Candahar. They had had to leave their dead littering the bloody scrubland, soon to be prey to the vultures and vermin.

Walker was too tired, too sick to his stomach to feel anger, pain or frustration. All he knew was that when he trained to be a doctor, it had been for the purpose of saving lives. It was not to watch young men's pale, bloody faces grimace with pain and their eyes close gradually as life ebbed away from them, while he stood by, helpless, gazing at a gaping wound spilling out intestines.

He needed a drink. Ducking back into the tent, he grabbed his medical bag. There were still three wounded men lying on makeshift beds in there, but no amount of medical treatment could save them from the grim reaper. He felt guilty to be in their presence. He had instructed his orderly to administer large doses of laudanum to help numb the pain until the inevitable overtook them.

As Walker wandered to the edge of the tattered encampment, he encountered no other officer. Of course, there were very few left. Colonel MacDonald, who had been in charge, had been decapitated by an Afghan blade very early in the battle. Captain Alistair Thornton was now in charge of the ragged remnants of the company of the Berkshire regiment, and he was no doubt in his tent nursing his wound. He had been struck in the shoulder by a jezail bullet which had shattered the bone.

Just beyond the perimeter of the camp, Walker slumped down at the base of a skeletal tree, resting his back against the rough bark. Opening his medical bag, he extracted a bottle of brandy. Uncorking it, he sniffed the neck of the bottle, allowing the alcoholic fumes to drift up his nose. And then he hesitated.

Something deep within his conscience made him pause. Little did this tired army surgeon realise that he was facing a decisive moment of Fate. He was about to commit an act that would alter the course of his life for ever. With a frown, he shook the vague dark unformed thoughts from his mind and returned his attention to the bottle.

The tantalising fumes did their work. They promised comfort and oblivion. He lifted the neck of the bottle to his mouth and took a large gulp. Fire spilled down his throat and raced through his senses. Within moments he felt his body ease and relax, the inner tension melting with the warmth of the brandy. He took another gulp, and the effect increased. He had found an escape from the heat, the blood, the cries of pain and the scenes of slaughter. A blessed escape. He took another drink. Within twenty minutes the bottle was empty and John Walker was floating away on a pleasant, drunken dream. He was also floating away from the life he knew. He had cut himself adrift and was now heading for stormy, unchartered waters.

As consciousness slowly returned to him several hours later, he felt a sudden, sharp stabbing pain in his leg. It came again. And again. He forced his eyes open and bright sunlight seared in. Splinters of yellow light pierced his brain. He clamped his eyes shut, embracing the darkness once more. Again he felt the pain in his leg. This time, it was accompanied by a strident voice: "Walker! Wake up, damn you!"

He recognised the voice. It belonged to Captain Thornton. With some effort he opened his eyes again, but this time he did it more slowly, allowing the brightness to seep in gently so as not to blind him. He saw three figures standing before him, each silhouetted against the vivid blue sky of an Afghan dawn. One of them was kicking his leg viciously in an effort to rouse him.

"You despicable swine, Walker!" cried the middle figure, whose left arm was held in a blood-splattered sling. It was Thornton, his commanding officer.

Walker tried to get to his feet, but his body, still under the thrall of the alcohol, refused to co-operate.

"Get him up," said Thornton.

The two soldiers grabbed Walker and hauled him to his feet. With his good hand, Thornton thrust the empty brandy bottle before his face. For a moment, he thought the captain was going to hit him with it.

"Drunk on duty, Walker. No, by God, worse than that. Drunk while your fellow soldiers were in desperate need of your attention. You left them… left them to die while you… you went to get drunk. I should have you shot for this – but shooting is too good for you. I want you to live… to live with your guilt." Thornton spoke in tortured bursts, so great was his fury.

"There was nothing I could do for them," Walker tried to explain, but his words escaped in a thick and slurred manner. "Nothing I could–"

Thornton threw the bottle down into the sand. "You disgust me, Walker. You realise that this is a court martial offence, and believe me I shall make it my personal duty to see that you are disgraced and kicked out of the army."

Words failed Walker, but it began to sink in to his foggy mind that he had made a very big mistake – a life-changing mistake.

London, 4 October 1880

"Are you sure he can be trusted?" Arthur Sims sniffed and nodded towards the silhouetted figure at the end of the alleyway, standing under a flickering gas lamp.

Badger Johnson, so called because of the vivid white streak that ran through the centre of his dark thatch of hair, nodded and grinned.

"Yeah. He's a bit simple, but he'll be fine for what we want him for. And if he's any trouble…" He paused to retrieve a cut-throat razor from his inside pocket. The blade snapped open, and it swished through the air. "I'll just have to give him a bloody throat, won't I?"

Arthur Sims was not amused. "Where d'you find him?"

"Where d'you think? In The Black Swan. Don't you worry. I've seen him in there before – and I seen him do a bit of dipping. Very nifty he was, an' all. And he's done time. In Wandsworth. He's happy to be our crow for just five sovereigns."

"What did you tell him?"

"Hardly anything. What d'you take me for? Just said we were cracking a little crib in Hanson Lane and we needed a lookout. He's done the work before."

Sims sniffed again. "I'm not sure. You know as well as I do he ought to be vetted by the Man himself before we use him. If something goes wrong, we'll *all* have bloody throats… or worse."

Badger gurgled with merriment. "You scared, are you?"

"Cautious, that's all. This is a big job for us."

"And the pickin's will be very tasty, an' all, don't you worry. If it's cautious you're being, then you know it's in our best interest that we have a little crow keeping his beady eyes wide open. Never mind how much the Man has planned this little jaunt, *we're* the ones putting our heads in the noose."

Sims shuddered at the thought. "All right, you made your point. What's his name?"

"Jordan. Harry Jordan." Badger slipped his razor back into its special pocket and flipped out his watch. "Time to make our move."

Badger giggled as the key slipped neatly into the lock. "It's hardly criminal work if one can just walk in."

Arthur Sims gave his partner a shove. "Come on, get in," he whispered, and then he turned to the shadowy figure standing nearby. "OK, Jordan, you know the business."

Harry Jordan gave a mock salute.

Once inside the building, Badger lit the bull's-eye lantern and consulted the map. "The safe is in the office on the second floor at the far end, up a spiral staircase." He muttered the information, which he knew by heart anyway, as if to reassure himself now that theory had turned into practice.

The two men made their way through the silent premises, the thin yellow beam of the lamp carving a way through the darkness ahead of them. As the spidery metal of the staircase flashed into view, they spied an obstacle on the floor directly below it. The inert body of a bald-headed man.

Arthur Sims knelt by him. "Night watchman. Out like a light. Very special tea he's drunk tonight" Delicately, he lifted the man's eyelids to reveal the whites of his eyes. "He'll not bother us now, Badger. I reckon he'll wake up with a thundering headache around breakfast-time."

Badger giggled. It was all going according to plan.

Once up the staircase, the two men approached the room containing the safe. Again Badger produced the keyring from his pocket and slipped a key into the lock. The door swung open with ease. The bull's-eye soon located the imposing Smith-Anderson safe, a huge impenetrable iron contraption that stood defiantly in the far corner of the room. It was as tall as a man and weighed somewhere around three tons. The men knew from experience that the only way to get into this peter was by using the key – or rather the keys. There were five in all required. Certainly it would take a small army to move the giant safe, and God knows how much dynamite would be needed to blow it open, an act that would create enough noise to reach Scotland Yard itself.

Badger passed the bull's-eye to his confederate, who held the beam steady, centred on the great iron sarcophagus and the five locks. With another gurgle of pleasure, Badger dug deep into his trouser pocket and pulled out a brass ring containing five keys, all cut in a different manner.

Scratched into the head of each key was a number – one that corresponded with the arrangement of locks on the safe.

Kneeling down in the centre of the beam, he slipped in the first key. It turned smoothly, with a decided click. So did the second. And the third. But the fourth refused to budge. Badger cast a worried glance at his confederate, but neither man spoke. Badger withdrew the key and tried again, with the same result. A thin sheen of sweat materialised on his brow. What the hell was wrong here? This certainly wasn't in the plan. The first three keys had been fine. He couldn't believe the Man had made a mistake. It was unheard of.

"Try the fifth key," whispered Arthur, who was equally perplexed and worried.

In the desperate need to take action of some kind, Badger obeyed. Remarkably, the fifth key slipped in easily and turned smoothly, with the same definite click as the first three. A flicker of hope rallied Badger's dampened spirits and he turned the handle of the safe. Nothing happened. It would not budge. He swore and sat back on his haunches. "What the hell now?"

"Try the fourth key again," came his partner's voice from the darkness.

Badger did as he was told and held his breath. The key fitted the aperture without problem. Now his hands were shaking and he paused, fearful of failure again.

"Come on, Badger."

He turned the key. At first there was some resistance, and then... it moved. It revolved. It clicked.

"The bastards," exclaimed Arthur Sims in a harsh whisper. "They've altered the arrangement of the locks so they can't be opened in order. His nibs ain't sussed that out."

Badger was now on his feet and tugging at the large safe door.

"Blimey, it's a weight," he muttered, as the ponderous portal began to move. "It's bigger than my old woman," he observed, his spirits lightening again. The door creaked open with magisterial slowness. It took Badger almost a minute of effort before the safe door was wide open.

At last, Arthur Sims was able to direct the beam of the lantern to illuminate the interior of the safe. When he had done so, his jaw dropped and he let out a strangled gasp.

"What is it?" puffed Badger, sweat now streaming down his face.

"Take a look for yourself," came the reply.

As Badger pulled himself forward and peered round the corner of the massive safe door, a second lantern beam joined theirs. "The cupboard is bare, I am afraid."

The voice, clear, brittle and authoritative, came from behind them, and both felons turned in unison to gaze at the speaker.

The bull's-eye spotlit a tall young man standing in the doorway, a sardonic smile touching his thin lips. It was Harry Jordan. Or was it? He was certainly dressed in the shabby checked suit that Jordan wore – but where was the bulbous nose and large moustache?

"I am afraid the game is no longer afoot, gentlemen. I think the phrase is, 'You've been caught red-handed.' Now, please do not make any rash attempts to escape. The police are outside the building, awaiting my signal."

Arthur Sims and Badger Johnson stared in dumbfounded amazement as the young man took a silver whistle from his jacket pocket and blew on it three times. The shrill sound reverberated in their ears.

Inspector Giles Lestrade of Scotland Yard cradled a tin mug of hot, sweet tea in his hands and smiled contentedly. "I reckon that was a pretty good night's work."

It was an hour later, after the arrest of Badger Johnson and Arthur Sims, and the inspector was ensconced in his cramped office back at the Yard.

The young man sitting opposite him, wearing a disreputable checked suit which had seen better days, did not respond. His silence took the smile from Lestrade's face and replaced it with a furrowed brow.

"You don't agree, Mr Holmes?"

The young man pursed his lips for a moment before replying. "In a manner of speaking, it has been a successful venture. You have two of the niftiest felons under lock and key, and saved the firm of Meredith and Co. the loss of a considerable amount of cash."

"Exactly." The smile returned.

"But there are still questions left unanswered."

"Such as?"

"How did our two friends come into the possession of the key to the building, to the office where the safe was housed – and the five all-important keys to the safe itself?"

"Does that really matter?"

"Indeed it does. It is vital that these questions are answered in order to clear up this matter fully. There was obviously an accomplice involved who obtained the keys and was responsible for drugging the night-watchman. Badger Johnson intimated as much when he engaged my services as lookout, but when I pressed him for further information, he clammed up like a zealous oyster."

Lestrade took a drink of the tea. "Now, you don't bother your head about such inconsequentialities. If there was another bloke involved, he certainly made himself scarce this evening and so it would be nigh on impossible to pin anything on him. No, we are very happy to have caught two of the sharpest petermen in London, thanks to your help, Mr Holmes. From now on, however, it is a job for the professionals."

The young man gave a gracious nod of the head as though in some vague acquiescence to the wisdom of the Scotland Yarder. In reality he thought that, while Lestrade was not quite a fool, he was blinkered to the ramifications of the attempted robbery, and too easily pleased at landing a couple of medium-size fish in his net, while the really big catch swam free. Crime was never quite as cut and dried as Lestrade and his fellow professionals seemed to think. That was why this young man knew that he could never work within the constraints of the organised force as a detective. While at present he was reasonably content to be a help to the police, his ambitions lay elsewhere.

For his own part, Lestrade was unsure what to make of this lean youth with piercing grey eyes and gaunt, hawk-like features that revealed little of what he was thinking. There was something cold and impenetrable about his personality that made the inspector feel uncomfortable. In the last six months, Holmes had brought several cases to the attention of the Yard which he or his fellow officer, Inspector Gregson, had followed up, and a number of arrests had resulted. What Sherlock Holmes achieved from his activities, apart from the satisfaction every good citizen would feel at either preventing or solving a crime, Lestrade could not fathom. Holmes never spoke of personal matters, and the inspector was never tempted to ask.

At the same time as this conversation was taking place in Scotland Yard, in another part of the city the Professor was being informed of the failure of that night's operation at Meredith and Co. by his number two, Colonel Sebastian Moran.

The Professor rose from his chaise-longue, cast aside the mathematical tome he had been studying and walked to the window. Pulling back the curtains, he gazed out on the river below him, its murky surface reflecting the silver of the moon.

"In itself, the matter is of little consequence," he said, in a dark, even voice. "Merely a flea-bite on the body of our organisation. But there have been rather too many of these flea-bites of late. They are now beginning to irritate me." He turned sharply, his eyes flashing with anger. "Where lies the incompetence?"

Moran was initially taken aback by so sudden a change in the Professor's demeanour. "I am not entirely sure," he stuttered.

The Professor's cruelly handsome face darkened with rage. "Well, you should be, Moran. You should be sure. It is your job to know. That is what you are paid for."

"Well… it seems that someone is tipping the police off in advance."

The Professor gave a derisory laugh. "Brilliant deduction, Moran. Your public-school education has stood you in good stead. Unfortunately, it does not take a genius to arrive at that rather obvious conclusion. I had a visit from Scoular earlier this evening, thank goodness there is *one* smart man on whom I can rely."

At the mention of Scoular's name, Moran blanched. Scoular was cunning, very sharp and very ambitious. This upstart was gradually worming his way into the Professor's confidence, assuming the role of court favourite; consequently, Moran felt his own position in jeopardy. He knew there was no demotion in the organisation. If you lost favour, you lost your life also.

"What did he want?"

"He wanted nothing other than to give me information regarding our irritant flea. Apparently, he has been using the persona of Harry Jordan. He's been working out of some of the East End alehouses, The Black Swan in particular, where he latches on to our more gullible agents, like Johnson and Sims, and then narks to the police."

"What's his angle?"

Moriarty shrugged. "I don't know – or at least Scoular doesn't know. We need to find out, don't we? Put Hawkins on to the matter. He's a bright spark and will know what to do. Apprise him of the situation and see what he can come up with. I've no doubt Mr Jordan will return to his lucrative nest at The Black Swan within the next few days. I want information only. This Jordan character must not be harmed. I just want to know all about him before I take any action. Do you think you can organise that without any slip-ups?"

Moran clenched his fists with anger and frustration. He shouldn't be spoken to in such a manner – like an inefficient corporal with muddy boots. He would dearly have liked to wipe that sarcastic smirk off the Professor's face, but he knew that such a rash action would be the ultimate folly.

"I'll get on to it immediately," he said briskly, and left the room.

The Professor chuckled to himself and turned back to the window. His own reflection stared back at him from the night-darkened pane. He was a tall man, with luxuriant black hair and angular features that would have been very attractive were it not for the cruel mouth and the cold, merciless grey eyes.

"Mr Jordan," he said, softly addressing his own reflection, "I am very intrigued by you. I hope it will not be too long before I welcome you into my parlour."

Dawn was just breaking as Sherlock Holmes made his weary way past the British Museum and into Montague Street, where he lodged. He was no longer dressed in the cheap suit that he had used in his persona as Harry Jordan, but while his own clothes were less ostentatious, they were no less shabby. Helping the police as he did was certainly broadening his experience of detective work, but it did not put bread and cheese on the table or pay the rent on his two cramped rooms. He longed for his own private investigation – one of real quality. Since coming to London from university to make his way in the world as a consulting detective, he had managed to attract some clients, but they had been few and far between, and the nature of the cases – an absent husband, the theft of a brooch, a disputed will, and such like – had all been mundane. But, tired as he was, and somewhat dismayed at the short-sightedness of his professional colleagues at Scotland Yard, he did not waver in his belief that one day he would reach his goal and have a solvent and successful detective practice. And it needed to be happening soon. He could not keep borrowing money from his brother, Mycroft, in order to fund his activities.

He entered 14 Montague Street and made his way up the three flights of stairs to his humble quarters. Once inside, with some urgency he threw off his jacket and rolled up the sleeve of his shirt. Crossing to the mantelpiece, he retrieved a small bottle and a hypodermic syringe from a morocco leather case. Breathing heavily with anticipation, he adjusted the delicate needle before thrusting the sharp point home into his sinewy forearm, which was already dotted and scarred with innumerable puncture marks. His long, white, nervous fingers depressed the piston, and he gave a cry of ecstasy as he flopped down in a battered armchair, a broad, vacant smile lighting upon his tired features.

the further adventures of
SHERLOCK HOLMES

THE WAR OF THE WORLDS

by

MANLY W. WELLMAN
& WADE WELLMAN

Mr H.G. Wells's popular book, *The War of the Worlds*, is a frequently inaccurate chronicle of a known radical and atheist, a boon companion of Frank Harris, George Bernard Shaw, and worse. He exaggerates needlessly and pretends to a scientific knowledge which plainly he does not possess. Yet scientists and laymen alike read and applaud him, even while they scorn the brilliant deductions of Sherlock Holmes and Professor George Edward Challenger.

Wells refers in his book to the magnificent and almost complete specimen of an invader, preserved in spirits at the Natural History Museum, but he carelessly, or perhaps even deliberately, overlooks the history of its capture, examination, and presentation. And both scholarly journals and the popular press almost totally disregard Professor Challenger's striking rationalisation that the invaders were not Martians at all. As for Holmes, he shows little concern over these injustices, but after consulting him, I have decided to put the true facts on record for posterity to judge.

When the invasion began, in bright midsummer of 1902, fear seemed to overwhelm every human being except the two wisest and best men I have ever known. On that Friday morning of June 6, when the first Mars-based cylinder was beginning to open at Woking to disgorge its crew of ruthless destroyers, I was hurrying to Highgate. Poor Murray, my faithful old orderly who had saved my life during the Second Afghan War, lay critically ill in his lodgings there. Even as I came to his door, newspapers and jabbering neighbours reported something about strange beings from Mars landed among the little suburban towns in Surrey. I paid scant attention, for I found Murray very weak and helpless. Almost at once I became sadly sure that he could not be saved, only made as comfortable as possible as he settled into death. Later that night, while I sought to reduce his fever, I half heard more news to the effect that the invaders were striking down helpless crowds of the curious.

If it seems that I was not fully aware of these stirring events that day and on Saturday and Sunday, I must again offer the reminder that all my attention was needed at Murray's bedside. From other people in the house I heard wild stories, which seemed to me only crazy rumours, that these creatures from across space had utterly smashed Woking and Horsell, had utterly wiped out the troops hastily thrown in their way, and were advancing upon London itself. By Monday morning, Murray's fellow lodgers and the people in houses to both sides had fled, I never learned where or to what fate. The entire street was deserted save for my poor patient and myself.

I could have no thought of going away, too, and leaving Murray. Day after day I did what I could for him, as doctor and as friend. Meanwhile, all about us whirled terror and fire, and, in streets below us, dense, clouds of that lethal vapour that has since been called the black smoke.

I heard the ear-shattering howls of the fighting-machines as they signalled each other above London's roofs, and several times I peered cautiously from behind the window curtains to see them far away, scurrying along at tremendous speed on their jointed legs fully a hundred feet high. It was on Tuesday, I think, that their heat-rays knocked nearby houses into exploding flames, but our own shelter had the good fortune to escape.

Through all this, Murray lay only half-conscious in bed. Once or twice he murmured something about guns, and I believe he thought himself back fighting the Afghans. I ranged all the other lodgings in the house to find food for him. It was on the morning of the eighth day, the second Friday of the invasion, that he died, and I could take time to realise that things had become strangely quiet outside our windows.

I straightened out my poor friend's body on his bed and crossed his hands upon his breast. Bowing my head above him, I whispered some sort of prayer. Then I went again to the window, peered out, and asked myself how I might escape.

I could see a cross street down the slope below. It was strewn with sooty dust left when the black smoke had precipitated, and I thanked God that Highgate's elevation spared me that deadly contact. Doing my best to see the state of affairs outside, I made out a dog trotting forlornly along a black-dusted sidewalk. He seemed to show no ill effects, from which I surmised that the vapour had become harmless when it settled. But then, just as I was on the point of going out at the front door, I saw a fighting-machine, too. It galloped along among distant houses, puffs of green steam rising from its joints. That decided me not to venture out in the daylight.

Again I roamed through the house, poking into every larder I could find. Some dried beef and a crust of bread and a lukewarm bottle of beer made my evening meal that Friday, with the silent form of poor dead Murray for company.

At last the late June twilight deepened into dusk. I picked up my medicine kit and emerged from the house, setting my face southward toward Baker Street.

A fairly straight route to my lodgings there would be no more than five miles. But, as I moved through the night toward Primrose Hill, I suddenly saw great shifting sheets of green light there. I had come near the London and north-western tracks at the moment, and upon the earth of the red embankment grew great tussocks of a strange red weed. I did not recognise. At least it would give cover, and I crouched behind it to look toward that unearthly light. I could make out fully half a dozen machines, standing silently together as though in a military formation. At once I decided that there was a formidable central concentration of the enemy, close at hand. Instead of trying to continue southward, I stole away to the east, keeping close to the railroad tracks.

Creeping furtively, I won my way well above Primrose Hill and saw grateful darkness beyond. I dared stand erect and walk beside the rails. But abruptly there rose the ear-splitting peal of a siren voice, a fierce clanking of metal, seemingly close to the other side of the tracks. In cold terror I flung myself flat into a muddy hollow and lay there, not daring to stir, while the monster came clumping fearsomely along, now here, now there. If it had seen me, I told myself, I was doomed. But it went noisily back toward the green lights. Scrambling to my feet again, I fled northward into the deeper gloom.

Today I cannot say exactly where my terrrified feet took me. I stumbled once or twice and panted for breath, but I dared not halt. I found myself fleeing along narrow, mean streets, and once or twice across open spaces among the buildings. When at last I stopped because I was almost exhausted, I judged I must be in Kentish Town. The houses there were deserted; at least, I saw no lights in them and heard no movement except the beating of my own blood in my ears. I sat on a step to rest, but I did not dare wait for long lest a pursuer come on clanging metal feet. Again I took up my journey. I came to a broad highway – Camden Road,

I decided – and fared on beyond it, more slowly now. Now and then I paused to listen. Nothing came in pursuit of me, but behind me to my right still rose the green glow from Primrose Hill.

When the early sun peered above roofs in front of me, I was among streets unfamiliar to me. This, I decided, must be Stoke Newington. I fairly staggered with weariness as I followed the pavement along in front of a line of shabby little shops and dwellings. One of the houses was half smashed, the front door hanging from one hinge. In I went, and was glad to find water in a pitcher, though there was no food anywhere. I drank in great gulps, and then lay down on a sofa, to sleep fitfully.

Several times during the day I wakened and went to look out at the shattered windows. No fighting-machines appeared, though once or twice I saw hurrying shadows across the street and the buildings opposite. This may have been the flying-machine that, as I heard later, the invaders had put together to quest through our heavier atmosphere. I finished the water and wished I had more when, at nightfall of Saturday, I went out and sent myself to go southward again.

Now and then I paused to get my bearings. I realised that I was moving east of Kingsland Road, and I took great care whenever I crossed a side street. Suddenly the sound of a human voice made me jump.

Glancing around, I saw a hunched figure in fluttering rags of clothing. He came toward me until I could see him in the darkness. He was old, with an untidy white beard. His eyes glowed rather spectrally.

"I thought that I alone was saved," he croaked.

"You, too, must have the mercy and favour of the Almighty."

"Favour of the Almighty?" I said after him, amazed at the thought. Not for days had I felt any sense of heavenly favour in my plight.

"The destroying angels of the Lord are afoot in this evil town," he said. "For years I have read the Bible and its prophecies, have tried to preach to the scoffers. Judgement Day is at hand, brother, and you can bank on that. You and me's left to witness it together, the judging of the quick and the dead."

I asked if he had seen any invaders, and he replied that they had been roaming the streets earlier in the week, "looking out human souls for judgement," but that for two days he had seen none except at a distance. Again he urged me to stay with him, but I went on southward. My course kept me on the eastern side of Kingsland Road for a number of crossings, until I came to where I could turn my face westward, skirting a great heap of wreckage, to head slowly and furtively for Baker Street.

At midnight, approaching Regent Street, I saw lights. They were white this time, not green. Hastening toward them, I judged that they beat up at their brightest from the direction of Piccadilly. But before I came anywhere near, I spied northward a gleaming metal tower – again one of the fighting-machines – and plunged into a cellarway to hide.

There I cowered, miserably hungry and thirsty, until Sunday noon. There was no sound in abandoned London. At last I slunk, like the hunted animal I had become, to make my way across Regent Street and move west along Piccadilly. I reached Baker Street at last, and saw no sign of destruction there. It gave me a faint feeling of hope. Along the pavement I walked, ready at a moment's warning to dive for shelter, until I came to the door of 221B. The familiar entry seemed strange and hushed. It was as though I had been gone for a year. Up the stairs I fairly crawled, then along the passage to turn the knob of the door. It was unlocked and opened readily. In I tottered, home at last.

There sat Sherlock Holmes in his favourite chair, calmly filling his cherrywood pipe from the Persian slipper. He lifted his lean face to smile at me.

"Thank God you are safe," I muttered, half falling into my own chair across from him.

He was on his feet in an instant and at the sideboard. He poured a stiff drink of brandy into a glass. I took it and drank, slowly and gratefully.

"You have been here all the time?" I managed to ask as he sat down again.

"Not quite all the time," he said, as easily as though we were idly chatting. "On last Sunday night, at the first news of disaster heading up from Surrey into London, I escorted Mrs Hudson to the railroad station. At first I had had some thought of sending her to Norfolk alone, but the crowds were big and unruly, and so I went with her to Donnithorpe, her old home. She has relatives at the inn, and they were glad to welcome her. News came to me there. On Monday, the flight from London moved eastward to the seashore, well below Donnithorpe, with Martians in pursuit of the crowd of fugitives. Then came comparative quiet with no apparent move into Norfolk. On Wednesday I returned here, cautiously, on foot for a good part of the way, to look out for you."

"I was with poor Murray up at Highgate," I said. "He has died. Perhaps it is as well to die, in the face of all this horror."

"Not according to my estimate of the situation," he said. "But to resume. I have hoped for your return ever since I reached here on Thursday evening. I have hoped, too, for word from my friend, Professor Challenger. But you must be hungry, Watson."

I remembered that I was. On the table was a plate of cracknels and a plate of sardines, with a bottle of claret. Eagerly I ate and drank as I told of my adventures.

"You have mentioned Professor Challenger to me, I think," I said between mouthfuls. "Just who is he?"

"One of England's most brilliant zoologists, and vividly aware of his own attainments. He would say, the most brilliant by far."

"You speak as though he is of a tremendous egotism."

"And that is true, though in his case it is pardonable. But do you remember a magazine article some time back, an account of an egg-shaped crystal that reflected strange scenes and creatures?"

"Yes, because you and I looked at it together. I do not care for its author, H. G. Wells, but I read it because young Jacoby Wace, the assistant demonstrator at St Catherine's, was concerned. He said that the crystal had vanished."

"So it had," nodded Holmes, his manner strangely self-satisfied.

"Wace told Wells that before he could secure that crystal from the curiosity shop where it had been taken, a tall, dark man in grey had bought it and vanished beyond reach."

"And what does that tall, dark man in grey suggest to you?" inquired Holmes casually.

"To me? Why, nothing in particular."

"Really, Watson, and you always admired my grey suit I got at Shingleton's."

I almost choked on a bit of cracknel. "Do you mean that you got possession of that crystal?"

"I did indeed. Challenger and I have studied it, and I left it at his home for his further observations. So, you see, we are not wholly unprepared for this voyage across space from Mars to Earth. When the first cylinder struck at Woking, a week ago last Friday, I hurried at once to Challenger's home in West Kensington. His wife said that he had joined the scientists at Woking, but I could not find him when I went there myself. I fear he may have been killed by the heat-ray, along with Ogilvy of the observatory there, and Stent, the Astronomer Royal."

"May I come in?" boomed a great voice from the passage outside.

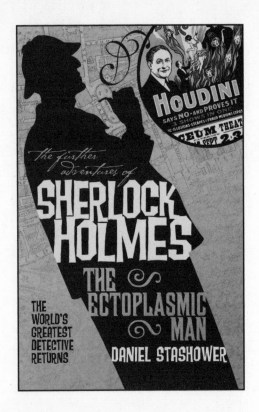

THE FURTHER ADVENTURES OF SHERLOCK HOLMES

THE ECTOPLASMIC MAN

Daniel Stashower

When Harry Houdini is framed and jailed for espionage, Sherlock Holmes vows to clear his name, with the two joining forces to take on blackmailers who have targeted the Prince of Wales.
ISBN: 9781848564923

AVAILABLE NOW!

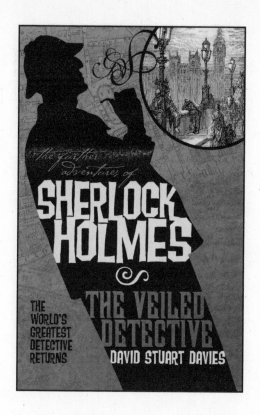

THE FURTHER ADVENTURES
OF SHERLOCK HOLMES

THE VEILED DETECTIVE

David Stuart Davies

A young Sherlock Holmes arrives in London to begin his career
as a private detective, catching the eye of the master criminal,
Professor James Moriarty. Enter Dr. Watson, newly returned
from Afghanistan, soon to make history as Holmes' companion...
ISBN: 9781848564909

AVAILABLE NOW!

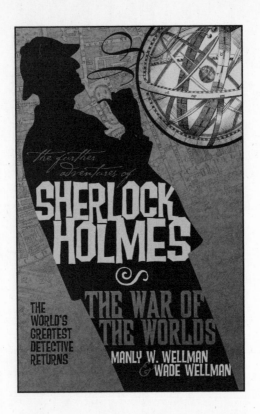

THE FURTHER ADVENTURES OF SHERLOCK HOLMES

THE MAN FROM HELL

Barrie Roberts

In 1886, wealthy philathropist Lord Backwater is found beaten
to death on the grounds of his estate. Sherlock Holmes and Dr.
Watson must unravel the mystery by pitting their wits against
a ruthless new enemy, taking them across the globe in search
of the killer.
ISBN: 9781848565081

AVAILABLE FEBRUARY 2010

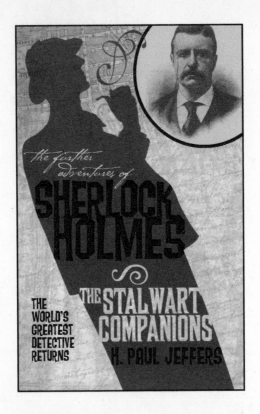

THE FURTHER ADVENTURES
OF SHERLOCK HOLMES

THE STALWART COMPANIONS

H. Paul Jeffers

Written by future President Theodore Roosevelt long before The
Great Detective's first encounter with Dr. Watson, Holmes visits
America to solve a most violent and despicable crime. A crime
that was to prove his most taxing of his brilliant career...
ISBN: 9781848565098

AVAILABLE FEBRUARY 2010